Gray Back Bad Bear

Gray Back Bad Bear
ISBN-13: 978-1517406080
ISBN-10: 1517406080
Copyright © 2015, T. S. Joyce
First electronic publication: July 2015

T. S. Joyce
www.tsjoycewrites.wordpress.com

NOTE FROM THE AUTHOR:
This book is a work of fiction. The names, characters,
places, and incidents are products of the writer's
imagination or have been used fictitiously and are not to
be construed as real. Any resemblance to persons, living
or dead, actual events, locale or organizations is entirely
coincidental. The author does not have any control over
and does not assume any responsibility for third-party
websites or their content.

Published in the United States of America

First digital publication: July 2015
First print publication: September 2015

Gray Back Bad Bear

(Gray Back Bears, Book 1)

T. S. Joyce

ONE

Another day working on the landing stripping lumber, another night at Sammy's Bar looking for *her*.

The one.

The mate that would fill the hole in Matt Barns's middle.

He touched the condensation on his half-empty glass of beer. A drop of water dripped down, gaining speed until it made a tiny splat on the napkin below. He and the water drop were on the same path to destruction.

The search was the only thing that kept his bear even, though, so he'd keep doing this—searching and failing—until his animal ate him up from the inside out. Until his alpha had to put him down when he'd gone mad. That's what happened to shifters like him. The bad ones.

He glanced up as the front door swung open. Two blondes and a brunette with bodies like goddesses strolled in on long stem legs. Matching cutoff jean shorts barely hid their asses as they walked toward a table near the stage. They looked around like they were on the prowl for trouble, oversize purses hooked in the creases of their elbows, and shirts so tight they were like a second skin. Lucky fabric. Two of them looked like they had fake tits.

Matt stood and downed his beer, never taking his gaze off a blond who'd locked eyes with him. Could his mate be one of them? Only one way to find out. He might be going down hard, but he was going to enjoy the shit out of the journey.

****

Willa Madden glared at the behemoth walking toward her friends. She'd clearly underestimated Brittney, Kara, and Gia because it was now abundantly obvious they weren't in Saratoga for a girl's campout like they'd been planning since middle school.

This was a werebear hunt. Her frown made her glasses slide down her nose, so she shoved them back into place primly. Shit on a cracker. She'd been hosed.

6

"Do you think that's him?" Kara asked in a rushed whisper. "It looks like him."

"Who's him?" Willa asked.

"Matt Barns," Gia said, flipping her long chestnut tresses off her shoulder. "He's on social media."

"Please tell me we aren't here for you to sleep with a shifter."

"Bucket list, baby," Brittney murmured, eyes on the approaching giant.

"Fan-friggin-tastic," Willa hissed out, angry at the epic dooping she'd fallen victim to. Her friends weren't even that smart, and they'd still managed to trick her into forsaking beach destinations for this hole-in-the-wall town.

She'd waxed her hoohah for this shit.

"You look tense. Why don't you go get yourself a drink, Willa?" Brittney asked ...*because clearly no one in here will buy you one.*

Brittney didn't have to say that last bit out loud. It was implied by her tone and her love of subtle dominance battles. She was queen bee, always had been, and Willa was the peon who was lucky enough to be invited anywhere.

Why had she put up with this crap for so long? Answer: she hadn't. She'd pulled away from their quartet in high school when their popularity rocketed to the moon and they didn't have time for her. But they'd all gone to the same college and kept in touch, and this was their follow-through on the blood pact they'd all made in seventh grade at Gia's tree house slumber party. Friends forever and a girl's trip after they all graduated college.

And somewhere in those five years at university, the three bombshells had grown an obsession with shifters. They'd stalked the Internet and signed up for alerts when any new ones registered to the public and...oh my God, she was so dumb for not figuring out sooner this was a shifter booty-call trip.

Three more men were approaching the table from across the room where the titan had been drinking, and now was the time to make her escape. She gave zero figs about shifters. *Leave the poor things alone* was her motto.

"Anyone else want a drink?" she asked as she turned around and shuffled backward in the direction of the bar.

"Nah, I think we'll get our drinks from these sexy boys," Kara said, winking at someone over Willa's shoulder.

She stumbled and ran into a solid brick wall. Or she thought it was, but when she turned around, Matt-What's-His-Face was steadying her with giant hands on her shoulders and a look on his face that said he hadn't even noticed her before now. Of course he hadn't. No one ever did when she was with the bombshells. "Oh, just great," she muttered, swatting at his hands. "Ignoramus," she huffed as she jerked away from him and stomped off toward the bar.

"Did you just call me an ignoramus?" the man asked in a deep timbre that sent a shudder down her spine.

"You best believe it, mister." When she cast him an angry glare over her shoulder, his eyebrows were lifted high and a surprised smile had curved his lips.

Piercing blue eyes followed her until she ran into something, a waitress, and toppled forward as they both fell. Willa's skirt flipped up, and she screeched as she hit the sticky wooden floors tits first. She was the worst at falling. She did it all the damned time, and she still had no instinct to catch herself with her hands.

"Oh, I'm so sorry," she groaned as she helped a dark-headed waitress shove trash and a half-empty basket of fries back onto her tray. "I'm such a clutz."

"I am, too. It's okay," the woman said. Her cheeks blushed bright red. "It's my first week."

"Oooh, now I feel even worse. You're doing a great job!" she called as the waitress bustled away.

"Hey, shrimp, can I buy you a drink?" Matt asked from above her.

From the floor, it looked like his head was touching the ceiling. "Shrimp?" Her mouth was so frowny it hurt. "That offends me."

Matt shrugged as if he didn't care. "It was that or Granny Panties."

"Granny Panties?" An exasperated sound huffed out of her mouth as she shoved the hem of her skirt downward to cover the panties in question. "They're called comfy cottons, I'll have you know. They came in six festive colors!"

"Oh, you smell angry. And you look angry, too, with your eyes all scrunched up like that." He was fighting an irritating smile as he offered her a hand.

"I don't need your help," she grumbled. "I don't need anything from you." She scrambled upward, still holding her skirt over her legs. "Not a drink, not a hand up, not a diddle, not a conversation. If it's a connection you're looking for"—she waved her hand over toward the bombshells who were in shallow conversation with the men from the bar—"they're your girls. The brunette is super easy."

She stomped off toward the bathroom.

"Really?" Matt called after her in an obnoxiously hopeful tone.

"No, asshole." She banged the single toilet bathroom door closed behind her and snapped the lock in place.

Puffing air out her cheeks, she slammed her palms down on either side of the sink and glared at her reflection in the mirror. Burgundy rimmed glasses, chestnut brown eyes, and dyed red hair. She'd even spent extra time on her make-up and straightened her hair with one of those flat irons the bombshells probably carried around in their purses for hair emergencies. Hmm, she did look angry.

She wasn't even mad at the shifter. Not really. He'd just caught her right when she'd felt betrayed by her friends. She was upset she hadn't dug deeper into the bombshells' reasons for visiting Saratoga, Wyoming instead of Cabo or Florida. Truth be told, she'd pathetically been so flattered at being invited, she'd sat back while they made the plans. Heat blasted through her cheeks. How stupid she must look to them. No doubt the bombshells had been snickering behind her back this whole time.

Why had they even included her on this trip?

A knock sounded on the door. Right, she was hogging the bathroom. "Just a minute." She washed her hands and re-adjusted her glasses, squared her shoulders because she was Willa-freaking-Madden, and despite how those girls out there made her feel, she was awesome.

****

Matt waited, arms locked against either side of the bathroom door frame. He'd pissed off the little human, but for the life of him, he couldn't figure out how. She'd had that smell about her that most women got right before they slapped him, but he'd gone over their conversation in his head three times and still couldn't think of anything he'd said that was slap-worthy.

"Matt," Jason said at normal volume from his stool at the bar. Matt could hear him just fine, but focused instead on the sound of running water in the bathroom.

"Matt," Jason called louder. "What are you

doing messing with that chick?"

Matt cast him a narrow-eyed glare as his bear snarled from inside him. She wasn't just some *chick*. She was embarrassed from showing her panties to the bar, and he was going to make sure she was okay. Or something.

One of the blonds was sitting on Jason's lap, ripe for the picking and practically unzipping his jeans in front of everyone. Matt inhaled the scent of arousal wafting from the bar. Why was he here, worrying about this girl who obviously hated him, when there were three ready and willing women in there with his crew?

The bathroom door swung open, and the tiny hellion ran into his chest. Again. Shoving her thick rimmed glasses up her nose, she glared up at him and blasted her hands onto her hips. She looked like a pissed off kitten.

Matt did his best to hide his smile, but damn she was cute in her little black skirt and red tank top with a miniature tie-dye purse slung across her chest. It was two short steps away from being a fanny-pack. Her make-up hadn't been slathered on like the other girls, but her doe brown eyes had been played up with some of that dark eyelid shit girls liked to wear, and her shiny red hair was pulled straight back in a ponytail and spiked out of the band, making her look like an anime character. She couldn't be an inch over five foot of compact, angry, nerd. Sexy geek chic, and the opposite of his type. Yep.

"They put these nifty pictures of girls in dresses on bathrooms in case you have trouble reading the word *women*," she said as she did a Vanna White at the bathroom sign.

Goddammit, she was cute all pissed off. "I made you mad." Wait, that was the best he could do for an apology?

Sexy Nerd sighed, and her shoulders slumped. "You didn't." She jerked her chin toward the trio of buxom beauties hanging all over his crew. "They did."

"You want to get out of here and talk about it?" Talk about it? He winced. Talking wasn't his gig. Banging relentlessly was.

"Ha! You, mister, are barking up the wrong tree. I'm a virgin and proud." She waved her hands in front of her skirt. "No one has touched this magical box with their tally whacker, and I assure you, you won't be entering my sacred temple either."

"Yeah, I figured. The pink polka dot granny panties gave you away."

"Comfy cottons."

He wanted to kiss that little angry moue off her glossed lips. Frowning, he said, "Well, you just saved yourself from my evil clutches because I don't touch virgins. I find them dissatisfying for my...needs."

When her face fell, a burning ache slashed through his chest. What the hell was happening to him? He needed to go find the woman who'd just about sunk her claws into him before he'd followed Sexy Nerd to the bathroom.

"You've been officially friend-zoned. The name's Matt Barns," he said, offering his hand for a shake.

"Oh." Her bravado faltered, and she looked vulnerable for a moment, then gripped his hand tightly and shook him once, hard. "Willamena Madden. People call me Willa."

"Willa?" He laughed. Even her name sounded nerdy.

"Yes, Willa. It's a family name. A lot of strong women in my lineage have carried that name."

"A warrior's name then?"

"Yes, you oaf. Stop making fun of me."

Matt cleared his throat and let the smile slip from his lips. "You're right. Where are my manners?"

"What kind of bear are you?"

"Now, where are your manners? Shifter etiquette one-oh-one. No asking about the animal side unless you know someone really well."

She wasn't paying attention and was instead clicking away on her phone. "Grizzly. Nice."

"What? How did you know?"

"I just friend-zoned *you*...on social media. Your About Me section is super informative."

"And what if I'd been a panda shifter?"

She scrunched up her face in a sympathetic look. "Then we couldn't have been friends, Matt Barns of the"—she looked at her phone again—"Gray Back Crew. I'm extremely prejudiced against shifter animals. Apex predators only on my friend card."

Matt snorted and pursed his lips to hide how truly amusing this little human was to him.

"Okay, while I have you here and talking, what size to you prefer?" she asked, digging through her colorful purse. She pulled out three condoms and lifted the tiniest. "Extra small?"

Shock jolted up Matt's spine as he

guffawed. "If you're a virgin, why are you carrying around condoms?"

"Oh, not for me. For them." She twitched her head at the Barbie trio. One of the blonds was now making out with Jason. "Safe sex is inconceivably important."

"I have my own condoms, thanks, and besides, you don't have the right size for me."

"Extra extra small?"

He gave her a cool look. "You're funny."

"I think so, too," she said through a giggle as she shoved the condoms back into her purse. "I'm glad you stalked me to the bathroom. I feel better now. Thanks, Griz."

Matt ran his hands over his face and shook his head. Willamena Madden was a handful in a tiny package. That was for sure and for certain. "Can I please buy you a drink now?"

Her eyes narrowed to slits behind her oversize glasses. "Why?" She slid her gaze to the left and right, then back at him. "Are you filming this? Am I being pranked?"

"What? No. I just want to hear more about how you ended up here. With them." He pointed to her friends.

"It's a long, boring story."

"I can't wait." And that was actually true, which was weird, because this was probably the longest he'd held a conversation with a woman without getting bored and popping off a dirty joke to shock her.

"Fine, but no trying to get in my pants. It's not happening."

"Wouldn't dream of it."

"And you also have to tell me why you passed them up to buy me a drink."

"So many rules, woman."

Willa crossed her arms over her chest, pushing those perky little tits of hers higher.

With a growl, he said, "Because I'm tired of banging shifter groupies, you seem to borderline hate me, and it's nice to laugh with someone instead of trying for a quickie fuck in the back of my truck."

Willa jerked back, her soft brown eyes gone round. "Honesty. That's nice for a change. Fine, Griz, you may purchase me a drink, so long as I buy us the next round."

"Why?"

"Because I'm a strong-ass woman who doesn't need a man to pay for my shit, and I don't want to feel like I owe you anything."

"Fair enough." He liked that she didn't need anyone. It would be the perfect friendship since he was infinitely undependable. Holding the crook of his elbow out, he smiled and said, "Pick your poison."

"Cranberry vodka," she said, chin held high as she marched clumsily beside him.

"Willa," one of her friends, the blond with the claws, said when they reached the bar. "I thought you were leaving."

Hurt slashed across Willa's face, and she hesitated.

Fury blasted through Matt as he leveled the obnoxious woman with an unamused look. He nodded his chin toward the door. "Why don't you leave?"

"Whoa, whoa, man," Clinton said from beside her. "Because we're having fun."

"Long island ice tea," Willa said to the bartender.

"Thata girl," he said, proud she hadn't backed down from her friend. He was well-versed in dominance battles, and anyone with any sense could tell Blondie was the ruler of her little human crew. He understood the need for putting less dominant animals in their place. He didn't, however, see the need for Blondie to send Willa off for no reason. These were supposed to be her friends, after all.

"Oh my goodness, there's a jukebox!" the brunette cried. She slurped down the rest of her drink and headed for the music maker in the corner, quarter held in the air tightly between her painted pink claws.

Willa introduced him to her friends, Brittney the alpha, Kara, and Gia was the brunette poking buttons on the jukebox.

"Matt the ignoramus," he said with an empty smile.

Willa snorted and choked on her drink beside him. "Yeah, about that. I was rude and shouldn't have called you names."

Gia clomped back to them on unsteady heels with a tipsy smile on her bright red lips. "Creed, dance with me," she said in a long, drawn out, whiny voice.

These women were usually Matt's exact type, so why was he turned off by them tonight? His dick had gone hard once, and that's when he'd watched Willa wave around the handful of condoms and talk about her virgin magical temple.

He laughed out loud. The nerd had got him hard where the Barbies had failed. He was going mad. It was happening now, his descent into insanity. His alpha, Creed, was going to have to put him down sooner than he'd planned. Fuck.

"You okay?" Willa asked, touching his forearm.

Matt jerked back at the burning sensation that blasted through his nerve endings where she'd touched his skin. "Sorry," he rushed out when he saw the hurt on her face.

The corner of her mouth ticked as her attention drifted back to the drink on the bar top in front of her. "Don't worry about it. I get that reaction a lot."

"Bullshit. That was all me. I don't like being touched."

Her eyebrows shot up, and she jerked her startled brown gaze back to him. "Why?"

Torture, scars, pain, dark madness, hurting everyone... "I don't know. I just don't."

"Well good, because I *hate* to be touched." Her eyes danced, and her teasing took the edge off the tension that sat in the air between them. "I'd rather lick a toilet seat in a port-o-potty at a construction site than get a hug."

"Seriously," he played along. "I'd rather lay face first in a fire ant mound than cuddle."

"Ack," she said, throwing her head back. "Exactly that. Good. Well, Griz, now we know where we each stand. No touching or this friendship is donezo. Deal?"

He chuckled and tinked his beer glass against her drink. "Deal." Damn, he liked talking to this girl. "So, how long are you in town for?"

"One week. We're camping out at the state park—"

"About that," Kara slurred from Matt's other side.

He stifled a growl at the interruption.

"Me and the girls actually made a reservation to stay the week at the hotel down the street."

"Wait, I thought we were having a girl's campout."

Willa's tone sounded hurt again, and Matt wanted to shred everything.

Settle down. She can take care of herself. She's tough.

"We just said that so we didn't have to feel guilty we'd picked Saratoga. You wanted to go to the beach, and we know you're super into camping."

"But...I brought the camper. Why would you help me set it up and not tell me you aren't going to stay there, too? I bought food for cooking out for all of us."

Kara scrunched up her nose and attempted to look remorseful. "You can stay at the hotel with us if you want to. You know I hate camping. The bugs..." Kara gave off an overdramatic shudder.

"Oh." Willa frowned and shook her head like it was no big deal. "That's okay. I understand."

"There's a pool at the hotel," Gia said helpfully from the other side of Creed. "It's kind of like the beach."

Seriously?

"Willa, you want to go to the beach?" Matt asked, surprising himself with what he was about to offer her.

She took a long pull of her drink as if she was trying to settle her emotions. "It's okay. It's not a big deal."

More bullshit. Her voice was shaking now.

"I'll take you to a waterfall that only the locals know about tomorrow. It isn't the ocean, but it has a sandy beach. We'll go swimming after I get off work."

"Ewey, that sounds amazing," Brittney chirped up. "I'd love to go."

"Invite only," Matt gritted out.

Brittney pouted her lip out and made her soft gray eyes really big. He imagined that look got her a lot of things she wanted, but Matt wasn't affected by womanly wiles. Not tonight.

"You know the rules, Matt," his dark-haired alpha, Creed, said, voice void of humor. "No woman on Gray Back territory."

"No, you said no potential mates on Gray Back territory." He tilted his head toward Willa and smiled. "Willamena here has been friend-zoned."

"Creed, she don't look anything like his type," Jason said, staring at Willa like she was a bug. "Matt ain't tryin' to hit that."

Jason was trying to help, but Matt still wanted to crack his skull on the counter.

"I don't want to be any trouble," Willa said, touching Matt's arm again.

She jerked her hand away and muttered an apology, but she didn't need to. Her fingers burned his skin less this time. Weird.

"Nah, you're right," Creed said. "It's no trouble. Matt can take you up to Bear Trap Falls tomorrow, but I'd appreciate it if you didn't tweet that shit. We like our privacy up there."

"I'll take the secret locale to my grave," Willa said.

Her voice rang with such honesty that Creed nodded his approval.

Matt released the breath he'd been holding.

He'd just made sure he would see Willa tomorrow.

Now he knew for certain he was going

mad.

TWO

Willa was sloshed.

Okay, in her defense, she rarely drank, and when she did, it was one glass of wine. Two long island ice teas, plus the beers Matt had ordered for himself but given to her, and she was three sheets to the wind and feeling invincible. She kissed her tiny biceps as she stumbled into the parking lot behind the bar.

"Steady there," Matt said, hooking his arm around her waist and pulling her from what felt like a ninety degree angle.

"This parking lot is tryin' a kill me," she slurred.

"I'm pretty sure you're the clumsiest person I've ever met in my life, Nerd. The parking lot is just an innocent bystander."

"Ha! You're a funny bear." Willa flung her arms around Matt's neck to stop the world from spinning.

"Jesus," he muttered, hesitating only a moment before scooping her up and pulling her against his chest.

"Oh, damn," she muttered, poking the hard planes of his pecs. "You're like a well done steak."

Matt snorted above her, but didn't look down. He'd been avoiding her gaze for an hour now, but she couldn't figure out why. "Are you hiding your eyes from me, Griz? Because they don't scare me, so you don't have to."

He lowered his gaze to her, his piercing blue eyes gone to a blazing silver color that should've terrified her, but she was too inebriated.

"It unsettles people, and I didn't want to frighten you."

"I'm not scared of anything," she sang out, stretching out one leg and tossing her arm back over her head.

"Clearly." He settled her into the front seat of his jacked-up Chevy and pulled the seatbelt over her lap.

"Safety first!" she crowed. "Oh, by the way." She leveled him a scowl. "I have a Taser. Don't try anything untowa...untoward... Don't try anything sexy with me, Griz."

"I definitely won't. You drank all my drinks, though, and now I'm completely and annoyingly sober. And I don't want you riding with your idiot friends, who refuse to take a cab."

"What time do you have to work?" she slurred, feeling dizzy again.

"I have to be on the landing at six in the morning." He looked at his watch and frowned. "So in four hours."

"Bad decisions all night long," she said sympathetically.

"You and me both, Nerd. You're going to be feeling this tomorrow."

"What's the landing?"

Matt shut the door and jogged around the front of his truck, then slid in behind the wheel and jammed the key in the ignition. The engine roared to life. "The landing is where I work. I'm a lumberjack."

"Gasp! You're a lumberjack werebear? That's so cute!"

Matt rolled his eyes heavenward and pulled out of the parking lot, but the smile on his face said he didn't hate her yet.

She stared at him to stop the truck from spinning around her. He had the body of a linebacker. Thick neck, baseball cap over his honey-colored hair, and eyes so blue they rivaled the sky. Well, before they'd gone silver. His nose was straight and handsome, and his cheekbones were sharp as glass. Across his strong jaw, he sported that designer scruff that looked like he didn't care, but the cleanly trimmed lines said he actually spent time looking this damn good. His tricep flexed as he turned off the main road toward a sign that announced the state park was five miles away. Unable to help herself, she touched his bulging muscle there.

"Do you work out?"

"Yeah. Some. Mostly my job requires a lot of physical labor so it keeps me in shape. Now, stop poking me and sit back."

"Right, touching is bad. I forgot."

He cast her a troubled look, then returned his attention to the dark road, illuminated by the headlights ahead of them. "It's not bad, per say…"

"Good, then feel my muscles." She flexed her miniature bicep as hard as she could and waited. "Come on. Touch it."

"Fuck, woman. Stop it." He adjusted his dick and draped his arm back over the wheel.

"Did my bicep just give you a boner?" She swallowed down the squeal in her throat.

"No." Matt rolled his head against the headrest like he was getting annoyed. "All the talk about touching did. Now cut it out. Just relax. I almost have you to the campground."

"You can't get boners over friends. It's against the rules."

"Tell that to my dick," he muttered so low she almost didn't hear him.

"Thanks for sticking up for me back there," she said, sobering a little. "That was nice of you."

"Willa, I'm not nice. Let's get that out in the open right now."

"Okay," she groused, crossing her arms over her chest. "You know, you don't have to take me to the Bear Crap Falls tomorrow. It's late, and you were drinking when you made the offer, and I know it was out of pity, and you will be tired from lumberjacking on no sleep tomorrow, so there it is."

"It's Bear *Trap* Falls, and there what is?"

"Your out." She wiped her hands together and flicked her fingers away. "You are free from your friend-zone obligations."

Matt swung his gaze to her, a deep frown marring his sexy face. "I'm still taking you, so I don't need that out."

"Oh. Okay. I did wax my hoohah so I could

look banging in my swim suit. Wait until you see it. I bought a sexy two-piece tankini with matching board shorts that cover as much as possible," she said in a phone-sex-operator tone. "It's polka dotted, like my granny panties, and baggy around the boobs. Does *that* give you a boner?" She was snickering on the last words and Matt's grin came back. Thank goodness. He looked downright dapper when he smiled.

"Thank you," he said.

"For what?"

"For getting rid of my boner." He laughed as he ducked her swat.

"I'll have you know I'm the subtle type of sexy."

"So subtle I can't see it."

"Lies!" she yelled, laughing. "I have a worm farm. Does that turn you on?"

"A worm farm?" he asked, turning right into the campgrounds. "So that's why you have dirt under your nails and smell like earth?"

"I stink?"

"Nah, you smell fucking delicious. Shampoo, soap, earth, and whatever flavor of lip gloss you've been slathering on all night. Cherry? Oh and..."

"And what? Finish it!"

"And you smell like arousal." He cast her a quick glance.

Heat flooded her cheeks. "That's not fair. You have heightened senses, and that is private information. Use your Spidey senses for good, not evil, Matt."

"I have an obvious boner that you keep pointing out. It's all fair, Nerd."

Touché. Leaning forward, she pointed out the front window toward the pop-up camper she'd bought second-hand a couple years ago. "That's me."

"Sweet," he murmured, turning in behind her Tacoma. "Is that one yours, too?" He gestured to the silver pickup. "Sure is, Griz. I use it to haul around my camper. Me and the bombshells had to take two separate cars out here, which is probably what saved my sanity." Were her words even making sense right now? She felt like she was floating.

"The bombshells?" He twisted in his seat and trapped her with those striking, inhuman eyes of his. "You never told me why you're on this trip with them."

"Because we made a pact as kids. Have you ever had a group of friends you thought were going to be together forever?"

Sadness pooled in his eyes. He looked

away and swallowed hard. "Yeah."

"Well, that was the bombshells and me. We were inseparable all through elementary and middle school and half of high school. Then we kind of...drifted apart. I think I was too different, and they couldn't understand me anymore. We'd always planned this trip, though. Right after graduating college, we were supposed to take a week long road trip together to someplace fun where we could just cut loose before we started looking for jobs in the real world."

"You graduated college?"

"Yeah, two weeks ago with a degree in fine arts. Hold your applause, you sexy giant." God, she hadn't meant to say that last bit. She pouted her lips and squished them together with her fingers, lest they speak on their own again.

Matt chuckled and opened his door, so she did the same. She nearly fell on her face when she slid out of the lifted truck, but bless her legs, they didn't fail her this time.

"You know," she murmured, punching the soft earth with the high heels she'd borrowed from Gia and trying not to break an ankle. "I used to feel sorry for you."

"What do you mean?" he asked, steadying

her waist as she aimed for the trees.

When she was back on track and marching toward the camper, she said, "I wanted all the humans to leave you alone when you came out to the public. I thought you lived these sad, lonely lives afraid of the humans, but you're not like that. I can't imagine you are afraid of anything. And look! Now you have shifter groupies to put your dick in all the time."

"Stop."

His voice had gone hard, so she turned and frowned up at him. "I don't feel sorry for you anymore is all I'm saying. You've changed my mind tonight." She splayed her hands against his taut chest, over his nipples which had perked up against the thin material of his charcoal T-shirt. Matt shuddered under her palms, and a soft growl rattled his chest.

Whoa, he was sexy. "You may ravish me now." She swayed but caught herself.

Matt gripped her wrists and plucked her hands off him. "Polite decline."

"Come on, Griz. This is what you do. This is your game. You lure shifter groupies here with your sexy selfies and witty one-liners on your social media pages, and then you sleep with them to settle whatever dark, primal desires your animal has. That's what everyone does nowadays, right? Boys sleep with girls and expect them to not get attached, and then they never call again. How many times have you done that? No strings attached fucking. How many times?"

Matt swallowed audibly and looked sick. Slowly, he shook his head.

"Ten? Twenty? If I don't jump on the bandwagon, I'll pass my prime and be an old, shrively-vaginaed shrew with nineteen cats and a pet pineapple. So here I am. A human telling your big"—she poked his chest— "bad"—she poked him again—"animal that he can have me."

"Don't," he said. He looked pale in the soft campground streetlight.

She stood on her tiptoes and kissed him. The growl in his throat grew louder as he grabbed the back of her hair and shoved her backward. Her shoulder blades hit the side of the camper so hard it rocked. Matt forced her mouth open with his and drove his tongue inside. A helpless moan escaped her as she wrapped her arms around his neck. Pulling him closer, she angled her head as he brushed his tongue against hers again. Holy hell, this was hot.

Matt's fingers trailed down her sides and

dug into her waist so hard, it hurt, but she didn't care so much about that right now. He was intense, and sexy, and she'd never had a kiss like this one. And that snarly animal sound in his throat was soaking her granny panties.

"No," he gritted out, easing back. "No, no, no. This isn't what I want." She nipped his lip, but he jerked away. "Stop it, Willa."

Oh, her real name. He must be serious.

The sting of rejection was fast and fierce. She yanked her hands away from him. "It's because I don't look like the bombshells, right?"

"No." Matt's eyebrows went up and his eyes pooled with honesty. "It's because I don't do virgins."

"Why?"

"Because I'm not the type of man who should be anyone's first. You'll remember it forever, and I'm not gentle or even that fucking nice, Willa. That's a lot of responsibility on someone like me. I'm not doing it. I'm not going to be the one who ruins your first time."

"You won't just try to be gentle?"

He shook his head for a long time. "That's not me."

Willa swallowed hard and pushed off the camper. "Goodnight, Matt."

She opened the camper door and stepped inside. She'd thrown herself at a man, and she'd still not been tempting enough.

Worst. Seductress. Ever.

Tears stung her eyes, and a sob escaped her as she made her way past the tiny kitchen space to the mattress at the end. Her duffle bag sat open, and she stared into the dark opening as Matt's truck roared to life. Their waterfall date was definitely off now. And when the sound of his truck faded completely, she grabbed her bag of toiletries and stumbled miserably out of her camper. The crickets and cicadas were at scream-volume levels as she walked to the public restroom down the road.

Teeth brushed, face washed, and glasses back in place, she ripped her gaze away from her blotchy-cheek reflection in the rusty-edged mirror and made her way back toward her campsite.

She froze when she saw Matt's truck parked in front of her camper. Perhaps she was drunker than she thought and hallucinating? But no, Matt was pacing in the dim streetlamp light. He stopped and hooked his hands on his waist, then glared at the camper door and muttered, "Fuck it." He reached the door in three strides, raised his hand to knock, then spun around and ran his hands through his hair as he headed back for his truck.

"What are you doing?"

Jumping, he said, "Shit. Why are you hiding behind the dumpster?"

In bafflement, she frowned at the smelly blue metal canister beside her. "I'm not hiding. I was just coming back from the bathroom."

"Oh." Matt was nodding like a bobble-head.

"And besides, you're a shifter. Aren't you supposed to have extra-sensitive hearing and night vision or something?"

"Yeah, but I was distracted."

She walked past him, her flip flops clacking with every step.

"Your pajamas don't look stupid," he muttered.

She looked down at her flannel shorts and white tank top she was pretty sure was too see-through for mixed company. But since Matt was obviously not interested in her nipples, she didn't try to cover herself up. "Thank you, I think."

"I want to sleep with you."

"That offer has passed, Romeo. I no longer

feel like the sexpot I did half an hour ago."

"No, I mean I want to lie beside you until you go to sleep."

She narrowed her eyes, confused. "Like a friendship cuddle?"

"Yes! Exactly that. Friendship sleeping. I've never done that shit before, sooo..."

"You've never slept beside a girl? What about all the girls you've diddled? And don't give me some bullshit like 'I've only been with two' because you and I both know you're a man-ho."

"I haven't ever just slept with a girl. If you accept my offer, you would be my first. Nerd."

She exhaled dramatically and gestured to the door. "Welcome to my humble abode. If the camper's a rockin', please come a knockin'. It means I'm choking or something and not actually having sex."

Matt's shoulders jerked with laughter, and he shook his head as he'd done a hundred times tonight. He seemed just as baffled as she was that he was back here again.

"Go on," he murmured in a deep, gravelly tenor. "I only have an hour before I have to head back to my place." He frowned down at a phone as he set an alarm, and then followed her distractedly up the stairs.

The bed creaked under his weight as he settled onto it, over the covers. Plucking her glasses from her face, he sighed and set them on the counter beside the bed. He lay down behind her, rigid as a mountain until she pulled his hand over her hips and cuddled back against him.

"Relax, Griz. I won't try to molest you anymore."

Matt's muscles softened, and he curled around her, spooning her like a pro. She smiled at the nylon wall and sighed as her eyes drooped with heaviness. There was a big old, scary-eyed grizzly shifter snuggling her, and she didn't feel anything but safe. That was kind of funny.

And just as she drifted off, Matt whispered, "You aren't what I expected."

THREE

Willa gasped and sat straight up. Sweat trickled down between her boobs, and she ran the back of her hand across the moisture on her forehead. What a dream. She'd been running through the woods from something big and always in the shadows, but she'd never seen its face. She'd only known it was horrifying.

The long rattle of a locust sounded from outside as Willa looked around. Had Matt really slept beside her? Perhaps not. She'd probably tossed all the covers at some point when she was running in her sleep from the dream monster, so there was no proof Matt's giant frame had ruffled the comforter behind her. And he hadn't left a single trace of proof he'd been there. Oh, wait. There was a folded piece of paper on the tiny kitchen table on the other side of the camper.

Willa tried to free her legs from the comforter, failed, and flopped onto the floor, but the future bruising didn't deter her from scrambling up and bolting for the note.

You snore.
Here is a list of touristy shit to do around town.
Microbrewery competition
Hot Pool
Art Gallery
Saloon
Here are directions for tonight. 6 p.m. be there or be square, Nerd. Bring an overnight bag in case you beg me to spoon again.

Underneath there was a hand drawn map and step-by-step directions to get to Bear Trap Falls.

She hadn't begged him to spoon, and she didn't snore. Did she?

She unfolded the last lip of paper at the bottom.

P.S. You don't really snore.

"Brat," she murmured through a grin.

Aw, Matt was like her own little personal werebear concierge, giving her a list of ways to enjoy her vacation. Screw the bombshells. She was going to make a fun trip of this without them.

****

Matt checked his watch for the hundredth time and muttered a curse that it was only three minutes past the last time he'd checked.

What was wrong with him?

"Get your head out of your ass and get back to work," Creed barked out from the top of the landing. His alpha was all riled up and pissed off about something, but hell if Matt knew what. Above him, Creed's dark eyes narrowed, and he spat before he jerked his chin toward the skyline hooks that dangled on the hill between them.

Matt couldn't even pop off like he usually did when Creed was being an asshole because this time his alpha was right. He'd been distracted all day. And working distracted on a jobsite like this would get him or one of the other Gray Backs hurt. Or worse.

He had to stop thinking about Willa. She was just his nerdy little sidekick friend who was going to point him in the right direction to which one of her friends he should bang first.

But that kiss last night against the camper…

Sheeyit.

A five-foot-nothing, smart-mouthed, pissed-off, lightweight, four-eyed geek was giving him a monster boner, and she wasn't even here.

Maybe he should stand her up.

His bear snarled inside of him, and the sound rumbled up his throat before he could stop it. Easton was up on a log tying a thick wire cord around the middle, but he turned his blazing green eyes on Matt the second the first rattle of his growl sounded. Double shit. Easton was crazy. Rule number one around a crazy grizzly shifter: Don't growl.

"Easton," he said low, hands up as he backed down the side of the hill slowly. "It wasn't a challenge."

"You growling at me, Gray Back?"

"Okay, technically you're a Gray Back, too, so that insult doesn't even make sense."

Matt crouched down as a massive silver grizzly exploded from Easton. Easton? His momma should've named him Beaston. Well, fuck it then. Matt hadn't had a good fight in at least twenty-eight hours, and this was an acceptable distraction away from his lady problems, so okay.

Matt closed his eyes and let the animal have his body. A snarling, ravaging bear burst from him as his skin burned from the ripping Change. Easton, the man, might be crazy, but he was no match for a bear like Matt's. Matt's animal had been forged from agony, taunted and tortured by IESA until the fear switch had been flipped off.

Matt's bear was a monster, and Easton was about to get some new scars.

He shook off the last of his ripped clothes as Eason charged down the hillside toward him. Matt caught the full force of him in the chest and latched onto his neck, sinking his long canines into his scruff until he tasted warm iron.

"Are you fucking kidding me?" Creed yelled from the ridge above. "Again?"

Hell yeah, *again*. He and Beaston hadn't managed to establish who was more dominant yet. Second in the crew should've been worked out long before now, but for whatever reason, they were locked in this constant battle.

Matt's footing slipped on the piles of felled lumber as he and Easton bit and clawed each other until their fur was matted with crimson. Stupid mother fucker didn't know when he was beat, and now part of his ear was torn and hanging off. This right here was why their bears couldn't figure out who was second to Creed. Beaston would fight to the death if Matt allowed their dominance battles to go on too long. He'd fight back until he was unconscious and bleeding out, and then wake up and be ready to redo the fight again the next day as though he hadn't lost.

Not that Matt was complaining. He loved this shit.

Matt raked a claw down Easton's back, but roared in pain when the other grizzly sank his teeth into his leg. Pulling, ripping, snarling, Easton pushed them both off balance with his powerful hind legs, and they fell onto a pile of loose lumber. Aw, hell.

Logs slipped and rolled alongside of them as they fought, locked up. Above them, Jason and Clinton were yelling something Matt couldn't understand. Pain blasted through him as a log landed on top of him and bounced down the mountainside. They were picking up speed, but Easton didn't seem interested in saving his own ass. He was still focused on maiming Matt. Attention torn between defending himself and making sure he and Easton survived the lumber avalanche, Matt twisted out of the way of another falling log, but got clocked on the neck by the next. On and on they slid, hitting tree stumps and brush, faster and faster. Pain, burning, agony, the *snap snap* of breaking bones. Fuckin' Beaston.

Matt swung around in time to see the lone standing pine at the bottom of the hill, but it was too late to maneuver away. Using all his strength, he kicked Easton clear and slammed into the trunk. His vision crumpled inward, and sparks shot around the edges as he curled in on himself to ease the pain.

When he opened his eyes, Creed was barreling down on them, massive grizzly body black as pitch and demon eyes to match. Dammit all, this was going to hurt.

Matt winced as Creed reached him, but his alpha leapt over his crumpled body and slammed into Easton, who was charging again. The snarling battle roars echoed off the trees, but Creed had this one. He hadn't won alpha from being a pussy. That bear could brawl. Matt would've huffed a bear laugh if he didn't feel like his bones had been ground to dust. Jason and Clinton were on him now, but were they concerned for the pain he was in? No. They were laughing. And pointing. And now

Jason was wheezing and clutching his knees because he found this all so goddamned funny. If Matt wasn't pretty sure his front leg was broken, he would have given them both a bear claw slap, but right now, his paw in question was bent at an odd angle and he felt like he'd taken a swan dive into a bathtub of hunting knives.

Creed was human again. His big dick he was always bragging about swung around as he jammed a finger at Jason and Clinton and raged. "This shit right here is why we don't hold a candle to the Ashe Crew's numbers! No wonder Damon Daye doesn't challenge us anymore. He expects nothing from us because all we do is fail him. Are you proud of that? Are you proud of sucking?"

"Kind of," Clinton said, his gray eyes dancing.

Creed reared back as if he'd been slapped. "Matt, Change back." The hard tone cracked with power and forced his immediate transformation. Alpha's orders could be brutal sometimes.

The roar of pain in Matt's throat turned into a scream as he shrank back into his human skin.

Creed grabbed Clinton by the back of the

neck and shoved him toward Matt. "You think it's so fuckin' funny? You set his bones back."

"Are you serious?" Clinton bellowed as their alpha stomped back up the lumber littered hillside.

The dark-haired alpha shot him a glare over his shoulder. "As a fuckin' snake bite."

They were all quiet until Creed was out of earshot, and then Jason said softly, "Some snakes aren't poisonous."

Matt groaned and wanted to kill them all.

"His bones, Clinton!" Creed yelled from midway up the hill. "Before they heal crooked."

"Fine," Clinton muttered. "Easton, Change back. You're half dead and the fight's over."

Matt couldn't see him from here, but Easton still smelled like a full-on grizzly and was growling softly in his throat.

None too gently, Clinton grabbed Matt's arm and started feeling around his broken wrist. Searing pain sparked across his nerve endings, but Matt gritted his teeth against the urge to yell out. The guys wouldn't have any sympathy, and besides, he'd had much, much worse in the Menagerie.

Still, bone setting was the least fun part of this life.

Matt loved the quick healing and the sex drive that came with being a shifter. He loved his strength and stamina, and hell, he even loved to Change. But bones had to be set before they healed improperly. Before muscles repaired themselves too quickly and had to be ripped up again to make sure bones fused back together like they should. He and the boys were all pros at bone-setting. Why? Because they broke them all the damned time.

Being a Gray Back was hell on the body.

Matt had enjoyed the fight to forget about Willa, but now, as Clinton snapped his splintered bones back into place, he thought of her to escape the pain.

FOUR

Saratoga's small town charm was growing on her. Willa smiled as she thought about the pottery shop owner who had shook her hand and talked to her as if they'd known each other for years. Here, everyone smiled at everyone, whether they were a tourist or a townie.

She tossed a look at the little brown bag sitting in her passenger seat and sighed. Matt would probably hate the gift, but that wasn't going to stop her from giving it to him. She'd spent the day at the brewery festival tasting tiny samples of beer, then window shopped in the downtown district before downing a personal mushroom pie from a local pizzeria that one of the nice brewers she'd met had told her she had to try. And then she'd wandered into a paint-your-own pottery place out of curiosity and bought a piece someone had left behind. Probably on account of its hideousness, but it was on the clearance table and reminded her of Matt. Not because it was ugly. Matt was extremely not ugly, but it was a mug with a handle shaped like a jumping salmon. And bears ate salmon. At least that's what she read in a pamphlet from the visitor's center about the sparse wild bear population around the area. She thought it was more a trout region, but the pamphlet had listed salmon as a grizzly's favorite food. With that knowledge in mind, she'd purchased the ugly mug from the pottery shop, two salmons from the grocery store, and thrown the smellier of her gifts into a cheap cooler packed with ice.

She was the best friend in the world. Suck it, bombshells, for not realizing her friendship potential.

Lodgepole pines lined the roads and filled the forest so thickly, she could barely see any brush on the wilderness floor. She drove curving roads edged with green and brown. Some of the trees were dead. A lot of them, in fact, but that had been explained in the pamphlet, too. Some kind of beetle infestation was taking over the forest here.

"Okay," she drawled out, pressing the map Matt had drawn against the steering wheel so she didn't have to take her attention away from the road to read the directions. A right turn here where the road was washed out to a well-worn dirt track, another mile winding through the trees that followed the tire marks, and then she was there. Her breath caught in her throat as she looked through the woods. Lush green gave way to a river. Even from inside the Tacoma with the air conditioner turned up, the babbling water was loud and beautiful.

She stepped out of her truck and pulled the backpack she'd brought over her shoulders. Shoving her glasses up her nose better, she hiked through the trees until she reached the water's edge. Matt had been right. This was sort of a beach, complete with pebbles that led to sand under lapping waves. The difference was the fresh water, the lack of brine scent in the air, and the bright greenery that lined the river on both sides. And no sharks. She could hear the waterfall, but she couldn't see it yet, so she hooked her thumbs through her backpack straps and tromped up an incline.

When she got to the top of the small hill, she locked her legs and halted.

Matt was sitting on the shore, water

lapping at his toes as he scooped handfuls of waves onto a burgundy stain down his side.

She was early by a half hour, and she hadn't expected him to be here yet. And she especially didn't expect him to be bathing what looked like copious amounts of blood from his torso. She backed up a foot, but a twig snapped under her flip flop.

Matt jerked his gaze to her. His eyes were churning silver, like mercury, and his face was bruised. He stood in a blur. "It's mine."

"What is?" she asked more high-pitched than she'd intended.

"The blood."

Oh. Well that made it better. "What the hell happened?" she asked, approaching slowly.

Matt scrubbed a hand down his face and shook his head. "Nothing."

"Bear shit?"

Narrowing his eyes, he huffed a sigh. "Yeah, bear shit."

She brushed her hand under a long gash across his rib cage, half-healed already. "Do you repair yourself fast?"

"Yeah. Give me an hour, and I'll look normal again. You're early."

"Were you hoping I wouldn't see you looking like a murder victim?"

"Ha." Matt's single laugh echoed across the river, and a smile brightened his somber face. "Kind of."

"Well, mission not accomplished. You look like shit."

Matt bent at the waist and scooped water over his forearm. It was then she noticed his skin. Crisscrossed in hundreds of long scars. His entire back was striped like a tiger.

"Matt," she said on a breath. Pulling his arm, she studied the marred skin across his ribs, then when he stood back up, over his stomach.

His face went hard as she studied him in horror. "I was going to put a shirt on to swim," he muttered as he crossed his arms over his chest, but that only exposed the scars across his six-pack abs. Pink and silver, each a different length and age from what she could tell.

"What happened to you?"

His eyes looked a hundred years old as he angled his head. "Nothing."

"More bear shit?"

He dipped his chin once.

Anger slashed through her, but it wasn't at Matt. It was at whoever had done this awful thing to him. Shrugging out of her backpack and tossing it on the ground, she said, "Falling off my bike, age seven." When he gave her a confused glare, she pointed to the crescent moon shaped scar on her right knee. "It was pretty awful."

Matt cracked a grin, and she could almost feel the relief roll off his shoulders. He didn't want to talk about what happened, and honestly, she didn't know if she was ready to hear what had ruined his skin like this. Already, she could feel tears forming and her throat thickening. She yanked her gaze to her discarded backpack so he wouldn't see how affected she was.

"What about this one?" he asked, gripping her arm and pressing his thumb against the scar on her elbow.

"Ha! You'll love this story. I was at band camp—"

"Of course you were at band camp—"

"Hush. I was at camp, and I was going head to head with Jenny Nador, who was such a bitch and always got first chair. I'd been trying for two years to get first chair just once. So we were up on this stage, and I was playing my ass off—"

"Wait, playing what instrument?"

"The flute, naturally. I am also a badass on

the piccolo. Stop laughing. So I'm up on the stage with my marching band, and my instructor has this smile while I'm playing like hell-yeah-she's-making-a-run, and I know I've got this. I'm going to finally beat Jenny Nador, and I already have my victory dance all planned out. I turn to shoot Stupid Jenny Nador a triumphant grin as I hit the last part of my solo—"

"Your flute solo—"

"Yeah, contain your boner. So then when I turned, the back leg of my chair slipped off the riser I was sitting on, and I fell backward, then out of my seat, then off the stage where I broke my arm in two places."

Matt let off a booming laugh and doubled over.

"I'm glad my pain amuses you."

"Holy shit," he crowed. "Please tell me your instructor gave you first chair after that."

"Third. I didn't finish the song, and then the ambulance came to get me and I didn't get to go back to band camp. I was heartbroken, naturally."

"You're the clumsiest human I've ever met."

"Yeah, well...you're the bloodiest bear-man I've ever met. Let's wash you off before I get queasy."

"Hmm," he said, lifting his chin. "I don't imagine you're afraid of much, Nerd."

"That's completely untrue. Wasps. Clowns. Open closet doors at night. Choking on a hot dog. Tight spaces. The dark in general. Stepping on hidden nails on the ground. Big dogs. Beavers, badgers, sharks, deep water, quicksand, the ridges in pickle slices, being ax murdered, dark parking lots, snakes coming out of the toilet, touching germy door handles after washing my hands in public restrooms—"

"Okay, I take it back. You're afraid of everything. Let's get you over one of them, though."

"Bears?" she asked hopefully, folding her glasses carefully and setting them on her backpack. She wanted to see his animal.

"No. Deep water."

"Oh, I'm not a strong swimmer."

"But you can swim, right?"

"I can bob."

"Well, why did you want to go to the beach then? It's a helluva lot more dangerous than a shallow river."

"I didn't want to go to the coast to swim in thirty feet of water, Griz. I wanted to lay out on the sand and drink pina coladas with tiny umbrellas and feel fancy. And go hunt for seashells and dig up some clams, and fish off a pier, and eat really good seafood. The bombshells had other plans, though. Speaking of...since you denied my virgin cookies last night, which one of my friends are you going to bone first?" Jealousy unfurled in her belly as she thought of Matt kissing Brittney. She didn't know why she'd just said that, and now she was fighting some epic heat in her cheeks, so she busied herself with taking off her thin cotton cover-up.

But when she looked back at Matt, his eyes were zeroed in on her yellow and white tankini.

"I told you it was hideous," she groused, embarrassed. "Stop staring at me like I'm awful. I'm already self-conscious about being in a swimsuit."

"Well, you shouldn't be." Matt's voice had gone husky. "Take those board shorts off though. You don't need them."

Mouth hanging open, she looked down at her swim shorts that were two sizes too big. They made her feel skinny. "But...my thighs are—"

"I swear to God if you say *big*, I'm going to

dunk you in the river. Take 'em off, Nerd." Matt turned and splashed into the waves, headed toward the waterfall. "Ain't no one out here to see you but me, and we've already decided to stay friends."

"Then why do you care if I strip down to my bathing suit? Hmm?"

Matt kept dragging his legs deeper and deeper into the water away from her and didn't answer. The ripped muscles in his back flexed with every step, and the perfect curves of his taut ass were now nestled in the wet navy blue swim trunks that clung to his body. Holy Toledo, he was the brawniest man she'd ever been with. Err...been friends with. Another wave of confusion filled her. She had to keep her head around this man. He saw her as some amusing little buddy, and nothing more. Last night, she'd thrown herself at him, and he hadn't taken the bait. She was more of a sleep-beside than sleep-with kind of conquest, and she needed to start learning her place with him now.

It didn't matter that she was harboring a teeny—miniscule really—crush on the mysterious, scarred-up bear shifter. He didn't feel the same.

Just friends. She could do this.

Willa peeled her board shorts off, grateful she'd shaved her legs past her knees today, and double grateful for the hoohah waxing she'd let some lady in a salon do before she drove to Saratoga. She stepped carefully out of her flip flops. Tiptoeing gently, she called, "Are you sure there's no glass in here? Fear number one hundred eighty-one. Fear of cutting my feet on glass."

"Stop being a pussy," Matt called without looking back at her.

"Okay, but that doesn't really answer my question." She took another tentative step onto the sandy bottom, and then another.

"Nerd, this isn't a public beach, and bears take care of their territory. Now come—" Matt shrieked, and his arms flew into the air just before he splashed violently under the waves.

"What's happening?" Willa screamed, running through the lapping water as fast as she could, adrenaline dumping into her system.

Matt wasn't breaking the surface to breathe, and the splashing was growing smaller as if he was being dragged under. She had to save him! "Matt!" she screamed, diving into the water. She swam as fast as her arms and legs could carry her, took a huge gulp of air, then submerged to try to grab him. Opening her eyes underwater didn't help much. She couldn't see thanks to the falls churning up silt from the bottom, but when her hand clamped on Matt's arm, he yanked her to him, and she could see him well enough. He was grinning, the pig-headed anus-cake.

She screamed underwater and blew out all the air in her lungs, then swam up to the surface. Gasping oxygen, she kicked hard enough to splash him in the face when he broke the surface. She headed to the shore, fuming at his prank. Not funny at all.

Matt was laughing, and she wanted to claw his sexy, infuriating eyeballs out.

"Nerd. Nerd! Willa! It was a joke, and look, now I know you can swim like a fish. No bobbing."

"Yeah!" she screeched. "I guess I can swim when I think my friend is *dying*. Congratu-fucking-lations on your epic discovery."

Matt's hands latched onto her arm. "I'm sorry. It was a bad joke. I didn't know you would get so upset. Wait, are you crying?"

She was, in fact, sobbing like a badass. Warm tears streamed down her face. "I thought you were going to die. I'm traumatized now, Matt!"

"Aw, Nerd, were you worried about me?" His voice was flippant, and she imagined he was like that with all the girls he met.

"Don't," she gritted out, touching bottom and standing to glare at him. "That little sarcastic attitude probably works with the girls you sleep with, but I'm not them. If something happened to you, it wouldn't just be a story I'd go back home and tell my friends. It would rip me up, you asshole."

"Hey," he said, grabbing her arm again as she turned to stomp out of the water. "I'm sorry. I didn't... I'm not used to people caring like that. I thought you'd let me splash around for a while."

"I thought a fucking crocodile was eating you!"

"Fear number one hundred eighty-two?" His smile was less certain now.

"It's not funny, Matt."

He pulled her against him so fast, she was shocked into stillness. "I like that you thought it might be a crocodile, and you still dove in to help me. Shh, no more crying. I'm sorry. I really won't prank you again. For at least a day."

"Har har."

"Do you forgive me?"

"You have a boner again."

"Oh good God, are you going to point it out every time I get one? It's unavoidable. You getting all protective is a turn-on."

Willa eased back, hands still splayed on his taut chest. "So I do affect you…sexually?"

Matt made a ticking sound behind his teeth. "Do you have a vagina?"

She gave him a dead-eyed look. "Yes, Matt. I have one of those."

"Then you affect me sexually. It's nothing personal, Willa. I get turned on easily."

He spun back toward the waterfall and began walking through the river toward it, leaving her near the bank.

And just like that, he'd reminded her that both her feet were still firmly planted in the unsexy sands of the friendship desert.

Up front, Matt stopped and turned, waiting for her to catch up. "Hey, remember that time you thought I was dying and tried to save me?" His obnoxious grin was back.

She splashed deeper and frog swam to him. "Yeah, but I learned my lesson and will never help you again."

"Still mad then?"

"Nope, just unaffected by your trickery."

Matt hooked his arms around her waist

and swung her wide as they treaded water. Waves lapped at his chin as he grinned at her with a cocky smile that probably got him in a lot of girls' panties.

The left side of his face was bruised but was already turning the green color of healing.

"Did you get in a fight?"

"With a tree or ten."

"So you got hurt while you were lumberjacking?"

He smiled like she was cute and pulled her around to his back until she wrapped her arms around his neck and held on with her knees squeezed against his ribs like a koala bear. Then he pushed off the bottom and swam them slowly up the current toward the waterfall.

Undeterred by him ignoring her question, she asked, "Is your job really this dangerous?"

No answer meant yes.

"Then why do you do it?"

"Because it pays the bills and keeps my animal sated. Kind of. I like the physical work, and I like my crew, and that's what we do. Each crew does a job. Some are construction workers, some firemen, some search and rescue. It's always something physical. Sitting around in a cubical would be equivalent to caging our bears."

She ran her finger across a long scar on his shoulder. "You ever been caged?"

"You're killing my boner, Willa." The words came out all growly and low.

"Well, perhaps that's a good thing," she said primly. "I don't even know if it's healthy to keep an erection for twenty-three hours a day."

Matt snorted and stood in neck deep water, the mist from the falls surrounding them. "That's why I go to the bar." He turned to her and trapped her in his blue flame gaze, as if he were gauging her reaction.

"Trying to hurt me by throwing it in my face how many women you sleep with? I'm unaffected, remember?" She pushed off him and swam on her back in a wide circle. "Besides, I'm quite scandalous, too. Once, I let Frankie Mercer finger me in my dorm room senior year of college. I even almost orgasmed." Her cheeks were blazing, but something about Matt made her want to say out loud all the things she normally wouldn't share with anyone. Perhaps because something inside of him had been broken, so he wouldn't judge. That much was obvious from his marred skin and his need for different women in his bed.

"Almost orgasmed? Frankie Mercer sounds like an amateur."

"Hey, don't say that. At least he tried. He didn't even ask for anything in return, just touched me like I'd begged him to."

Matt stopped treading water and stood, the water coming up to the tight buds of his nipples. "You begged?"

"Told you I was scandalous. Now, why haven't you accepted my friend requests on your social media pages?"

A deep frown darkened Matt's features. "I don't know."

"Bullshit, you do. Since we're friends, I think we should be honest with each other. We could play games if we were trying to date, but we aren't, so let's have it. Why not?"

Matt's chest rose with his deep inhalation. "Because I don't really want you to see the comments on my pages."

"You're afraid I'll look at you differently if I discover you are a man-ho? I've already accepted that."

"Yeah, but convincing yourself to accept that about me will be harder if you see what the girls I've been with post on my walls."

"Right. Only show me your best side then."

"You're only here for a week, Willa. I'd rather have fun getting to know you before you judge me based on—"

"Your actions?"

"Yeah," he said darkly. Gulping a breath, he turned, dove under the water, and didn't come up again until he was on the other side of the waterfall against the cliff.

He wanted to get to know her? Warmth pooled in her stomach and drew a small smile from her lips. She interested him on some level. Her, Willamena Madden, awkward, clumsy, piccolo-playing human who was shite at swimming and an unintentional prude to boot, had captured the curiosity of an infinitely sexy, playboy grizzly shifter.

Unable to stifle her curiosity, she asked, "Have you ever brought a girl up here before?"

"No," he answered easily as he shook his hair out like a Labrador.

The heat in her middle turned molten, and she clutched her stomach to settle the butterflies that had made a home there.

Stretching out her toes, she was barely able to stand on a rock under the water. She let the edge of the waterfall pour over her outstretched fingers. It was more powerful than she'd imagined, and she laughed as the sting made her yank her hand back.

"Come here. This part is gentler," Matt said, watching her with those smiling, intense eyes. He always seemed to be studying her reaction to everything.

Holding her breath, she swam under the falls, deeper and deeper. She looked up at the bubbles all around her, the light streaming through the murky water like sunrays. It was beautiful under here. Serene even.

Matt jumped in and paddled his hands upward, sinking down beside her. Tiny bubbles clung to his cheeks, and she brushed one off and searched his bright blue eyes. Under here, the world didn't matter. Here, it was bubbles, burning lungs, and the power of the waterfall vibrating against their skin. She reached out and touched a stripe across his chest, and before she could chicken out, she swam forward and brushed her lips against it, then kicked her legs for the surface on the other side of the falls.

Matt took longer to break the water, but perhaps she'd shocked him. She didn't know. When he pushed himself up on the rock she had sat on, his face was carefully composed. "What was that for?"

"It was because I don't mind your scars. I

don't know what caused them, but it doesn't matter to me." She nodded her chin decidedly. "You still look fuckin' awesome."

Matt released a shaky breath, the first proof he wasn't as immovable as he let on. Leaning back, locking his elbows on the craggy rock under them, he said, "You look fuckin' awesome, too."

She waited for the punchline, but he didn't give one. Instead, he looked out thoughtfully at the underside of the waterfall and let her keep the compliment.

With a happy sigh, she laid back and rested the back of her head on her crossed arms, then splashed her feet languidly under the gentle streams of water that fell near them. "Are there weremermaids?"

Matt laughed and hooked his foot under hers, then lifted it out of the water. "Why? Do you want to be one?"

"Maybe. My skin wouldn't prune if I was a mermaid. Look at this." She held up her fingertips and showed him her water-logged wrinkles there.

"You know, if you were a shifter, you wouldn't have to wear glasses anymore. Your vision would be scary good."

"Please, you would miss my sexpot

glasses."

"I would, actually. You have that sexy librarian look going on. I dig it."

"Ha, I doubt it. I heard your crew last night. I'm not your type. I imagine you don't take many girls like me to your love shack."

"Nope," he agreed, lifting her foot out of the water with his again.

"Keep doing that," she encouraged. "I like playing footsies with a werebear."

Matt snorted. "Bear shifter."

"So to become a bear shifter, I'd have to what? Let you drink my blood or something?"

"I'm not a vampire, and no. A deep bite would do it."

"You ever bitten anyone before?"

His eyebrows arched up, and the smile dipped from his face as he let her foot splash back into the water. "You mean have I Turned anyone? Hell no. I'm an asshole, but I wouldn't ruin anyone's life like that. Putting an animal in someone isn't a gift, Willa. It's cursing them."

"Sounds pretty awesome, though. Getting to change into this big strong animal, never getting bullied, always feeling like a badass."

"Mmm," he said noncommittally. "You were bullied?"

"You mean in school? College no, because no one cares what kind of freak flag you fly there, but in high school...you know, it might surprise you, but I wasn't the put-together vixen you see before you." She gave him a smile to let him know she was teasing.

"Braces?"

"Oh, yeah. Headgear. My teeth looked like old cemetery headstones. And my parents didn't have much money, so when we figured out my vision sucked, my mom bought me some glass frames from one of those old thrift stores and had some lenses put in them, so I was rocking grandma glasses until I was a sophomore. I picked up a job tutoring middle school kids on the weekends just to purchase a snazzier pair. As you can imagine, an updated pair of glasses didn't really stop the teasing."

"Kids can be jerks at that age," he said in a faraway voice.

"What about you? Were you the cool kid in school? Wait, wait, wait, let me guess. You were built like an eighteen-wheeler even in high school, so your coach recruited you early and you were star of your football team, taking them all the way to state by your senior year. You spent the entirety of your last year in high school smelling like cheerleader poon and managed to win homecoming and prom king. Am I close?"

Matt pursed his lips as the smile faded from his eyes. "I didn't go to school."

"You didn't go to college?"

"No, I mean, I didn't go to high school or middle school. I'm self-educated." He frowned. "Kind of."

Willa sat up, shocked to her core. "I don't understand. So you did homeschool?"

"No, Willa." A strange humming growl emanated from his chest. "I mean not everyone gets to go to school. Maybe for humans it's easier, but for me and the kids I lived with, it wasn't doable. We lived out in the woods in this shitty RV I found us, and I worked three jobs to keep us fed. There wasn't a lot of time leftover for school. I was a kid raising kids."

"What about your parents?"

"Stop looking at me like that."

"Like what?" Shocked and horrified because the stuff he was telling her pointed to a long life of pain, and fun-loving Matt didn't fit the bill for a wrecked life.

"Like you pity me. Fuck." He shook his head and looked away, but she'd already seen it. His eyes had lightened to that inhuman silver color. "Don't ask me questions like these anymore. One week, remember? I don't want to talk about anything—"

"But maybe you should—"

"Not with you! I'm not keeping secrets because I've had some hard life I can't come to grips with, Willa. I've talked to my friend, Kong. Told him everything. I know the dangers of keeping shit like that inside, and I didn't do it. But with you... Don't you get it? I just want to have fun. I don't want the serious shit I have to deal with when I talk to my crew or my friends. I want things to be light with you. Easy." Matt slid an angry glare to her. "I want to be someone else with you."

Willa bit her lip and nodded until her words found her again. "Okay. Easy. I can do that."

"Good." Matt pushed off the rock and dove under the falls. The sunlight glinted off the silver spider webs of his scarred back as he swam just under the surface of the water and away from her, blurring as he escaped the edge of her good vision.

She unclenched her hands that she hadn't realized she'd gripped into fists, and her heart ached. Matt wasn't interested in her, or even interested in being friends.

He only wanted to escape himself for a little while with someone who didn't know him.

FIVE

Too far away for Willa's blurry eyes to see, there was splashing and chaos on the shore where Matt was headed. They weren't alone in this magic place under the waterfall anymore.

Confused and a little gut-hurt, Willa slipped off the rock and back under the falls. As she swam closer to the shore and the people there became clearer, her stomach sank with every stroke.

Brittney's high-pitched flirty laugh echoed across the water, drawing a wince from Willa. And when she stepped clumsily onto the shore, her tankini clinging to her like an ill-fitting second skin, Brittney was hanging from Matt's neck, whispering in his ear while he held her elbows and listened with a faraway look in his eyes. Great.

"Hey again," Jason said with a friendly

smile. "Sorry we crashed the party, but these three were relentless to come up here."

"I thought you said no potential mates up here," Matt said to one of his crew mates. Creed, she remembered him calling the dark-haired, dark-eyed man from last night.

"We're not potential mates," Kara said, peeling her tank top off to expose her perfectly perky boobs nearly bobbing out of her purple teeny bikini. "Potential bed-mates only," she said with a wink at Jason.

Jason growled low in his throat and nipped at her neck, then jerked his chin toward the water and took off. Kara followed, giggling loudly.

"That's an awesome bathing suit," Brittney said as she peeled her beach dress off to expose her perfect ten body, barely contained in her bikini. "I think my grandma has the same one."

Cheeks heating, Willa jerked her gaze to the water so Matt wouldn't see how bad Brittney's insults stung. Really, she should be used to it by now.

"I saw your post online," Brittney said to Matt. "This place sounded amazing so we just had to come check it out for ourselves."

"Wait, you accepted her friend request but

not mine?" Willa's voice came out high and hurt.

Brittney snorted as Matt seemed to struggle to find his words. "Okay, why is that shocking to you?" she asked Willa as she passed. "Come on, Matthew. I want to see the waterfall."

Matt ran his hands over his wet hair, spiking it up in all directions. "I can tell by the look on your face you're figuring out I was telling the truth," he murmured as he walked by. "I'm not a nice guy." He brushed her hip with a light touch of his fingertips as his gaze followed Brittney. "I'm sorry if you got hurt."

"That's fine," she said, unable to hold his gaze. She looked down at her feet in the sand instead. She ghosted a glance up to him and looked back down before he saw her eyes brimming with stupid tears. "It's my fault for thinking you had more substance."

Matt flinched, but left her standing there as he walked purposely into the water after the bombshells, who were splashing and laughing with Jason and a blond guy she recognized from the bar last night.

She slipped into her board shorts and glasses and pulled her oversize cover-up over her head. Smiling politely at Creed, she pulled her backpack over her shoulders.

"Nah, you can't leave now," Creed said, sympathy in his dark eyes. "Come on over here and sit with me. I hate swimming."

Gia yelled, "Creed, come on!" but the man shook his head and dug a pair of beers out of a red cooler someone had set in the sand.

He popped the top on both of them and handed her one.

"Why don't you like swimming?" Willa asked, settling down into a forest green bag chair.

Creed's eyes tightened, and he shook his head. "I just don't."

Awesome. More mysteries. Why couldn't anyone just give a fucking straight answer around here? To mask the very pathetic, human growl clawing its way up her throat, she took a ridiculously long swig of beer. Watching Brittney chase Matt with long, graceful strokes through the water made Willa regret staying. Maybe if she drank her beer faster, she could excuse herself and go back to the campground to nurse her heart wounds in private.

Why were the bombshells getting to her like this? It's not like they were doing anything out of character. It had obviously upset

Brittney last night when Matt invited Willa out here instead of her, so of course she would've manipulated the rest of his crew into bringing them out to Bear Trap Falls. It wasn't even about Matt. Willa already knew what the future held, like a freaking psychic. Brittney would chase Matt until he gave in, which would probably take all of three point eight seconds, she'd sleep with him, and then she'd gloat in front of Willa every chance she got. She'd done the same thing to Paul Dunner freshmen year of high school and Seth Mayor a year later. And they weren't even friends then. It was some sick game Brittney played to make sure Willa still knew her place. She'd learned quickly to hide any crushes on boys because they would inevitably end up on Brittney's long list of conquests.

"I don't know why I'm still stuck in high school," she murmured.

"What?" Creed asked. "Y'all are legal, right?"

"Oh, good God," she muttered. "Yeah, we're all college graduates and plenty legal. Do you ever feel like you're stuck in some immature drama that you just can't escape?"

Creed gave Jason a hard glare and drawled out, "Yep."

"Well, that's me and the bombshells." She downed the rest of her beer and handed him the empty. "Creed, it's been real. I think it's high time I bowed out of the drama, though."

"You're better than them, you know?" He looked up from his own bag chair with serious eyes.

"Nah." She hoisted her backpack onto her shoulders. "I'm not trying to be better than anyone. I'm just trying to be better than I was yesterday. See you around."

Creed smiled and lifted his half empty beer. "Later."

"What, you're not even going to say goodbye?" Brittney called in a pouty voice.

Willa flipped that canker blossom the bird over her shoulder and made her way through the trees in the direction of her truck. She kicked a limb off the trail and fought the urge to try and break it in half for good measure. She had scrawny arms and no muscle tone, so it would just give her splinters and a bicep spasm.

And why were her stupid tears trying to escape again? Stupid Matt and stupid Brittney and stupid—"

"I hated that."

With a gasp, Willa skidded to a stop and

clutched her chest as if it would keep her heart from leaping out through her rib cage. Great gads, Matt was fast.

He stood leaned against her truck, arms crossed over his bare chest, navy swim trunks hanging low, still dripping wet with river water.

"Hated what?" she gritted out, pushing by him to throw open the door and toss her backpack inside.

Matt scratched his neck, then pulled her into a spine crushing hug. "I don't like Brittney. I don't want Brittney."

Willa struggled against him, beating his chest with her closed fists and screeching. "Then why did you act like you couldn't get away from me fast enough?"

"Because I want to take this slow! Fuck, Willa. I want to take things slow. You aren't like the others. Not to me. Stop." He gripped her pounding wrists. "Stop!"

A sob wrenched from her throat, and she threw herself backward until her shoulders slammed against the bed of the truck. "Don't touch me."

Matt let off a humorless laugh. "That's supposed to be my line."

"So Brittney gets to see the real you, but I

don't."

"Because I want you to see me as I am. Not the stupid persona I've used to…"

"To what? Say it, Matt."

He gripped his hair and then flung his hands forward. "To seem normal!" He backed up against the truck and slid down. Sitting in the dirt, he pressed the heels of his hands against his eyes and rasped out. "I wanted you to stick around long enough to get to know the real me, and if I accept your friend request, you'll see what an asshole I've been."

"Full disclosure or I'm leaving, and I'm not coming back, Matt."

"I know. And you should know everything. I just didn't want you to." He swallowed hard and pulled a cell phone from a canvas bag beside him. He punched some buttons and said, "There. Please don't hate me."

Willa yanked her cell phone from her backpack and strode around Matt to the back of the truck. She pulled the tailgate down and sat, settling against the hard metal. Was she strong enough for this? She liked the Matt she'd gotten to know, but was she going to feel the same after she saw whatever he was afraid of showing her?

His social media wall was bombarded with

pictures of him with other girls. In some, his eyes were glossed over as if he'd been drinking. In others, he was clear and smiling. The happiness never reached his eyes in those, though. All of the women were beautiful, but after scrolling a while, they all looked the same. Matt certainly had a type. There were videos of him making out with women at Sammy's bar. One of him doing karaoke with a set of gorgeous twins who did a triple kiss with him at the end. Willa's stomach curdled, and she felt sick.

In another video, one of his crewmates—Jason?—had walked in on Matt in the bathroom at Sammy's bar with his jeans lowered to halfway down his ass as he tried to cover up a girl he was obviously fooling around with. Matt said, "Come on, man. This is sacred." He put his big hand over the camera lens, but the entire time, he and Jason were laughing.

More selfies of women biting his ear, arms around his neck, a video of him skinny dipping in a steaming pool with a bevy of beauties. Hashtag spring break. Hashtag did a werebear. Hashtag bucket list.

Just like the bombshells had come for, Matt had given into so many others.

Warm tears streaked down her cheeks and landed with soft splats against her board shorts.

"What are you searching for, Matt?" Her voice came out broken and sad.

"A mate."

"Is sex an addiction for you?"

"No." He stood and locked his hands on either side of her hips, rocking the truck with the force of it. "Willa, it's not like that. I know the difference. My sister...shit." He took a deep breath and tried again. "This isn't every night or every week. Those posts are the highlight reel. My bear needs a mate, or I'm going to lose my mind."

"Matt, be serious."

"I am! I am being serious. He's never been right. My animal is wild and wants to fight everything, all the time, and I can feel my control slipping with each year. I've seen it happen—seen a dominant bruin go mad because he loses control of his animal. I want a mate."

"As a hail mary to save yourself from insanity? And what if that doesn't work? Where will that leave your mate?"

"It will work, Willa. You have to trust me, it will. I can already feel it working."

She drew back and froze, eyes wide. "What do you mean?"

"It's you."

Her face crumpled, and she couldn't hold his blue gaze any longer. "What do you mean it's me?"

"You're my mate."

"Aw, fuck off, Matt. I don't want to play this game." She shoved him back and slid off the tailgate, then slammed it closed as fury pounded through her. He had some nerve.

"It's not a game, Willa, I swear. I knew at the bar, the first time I talked to you."

"You didn't even notice me until I ran into you! And you just left me to go swim with Brittney. I don't know how this mate stuff works, but I'm pretty sure you aren't supposed to be chasing other tail. Are you even capable of monogamy?"

"Yes! I haven't even thought of another woman since I've met you."

"For one whole day you haven't thought of another woman."

"This is why I wanted to take things slow, Willa. It's instant for me. Dammit, I thought I'd never find you, but now my bear is ripping me up from the inside out because I made you cry. I know it's not the same for humans, though, so I thought if we could just date, and you could see how happy I can make you, you'd give us a chance."

"But..." She thought of all the drop-dead gorgeous women he'd been with. "I'm not your type."

"You're exactly my type."

"Fearful nerd is your new thing?"

Matt let off a surprised laugh. "Yeah. I guess so."

"I'm leaving to go back to my life in Louisiana in a week," she said softly. "I'm going to get a job and go back to my apartment and my worm farm and live a normal life."

"Well, I was hoping to court you into sticking around here a little longer. We can bring your worm farm here. I can build you one as big as you want. We have room for everything where I live. Worm farms, gardens, space to play your instruments...whatever would make you happy. I had all these plans."

She tried to stifle her smile as the flutters in her stomach picked up again. "What sort of plans?"

His tone dipped low to a seductive purr. "I'm going to show you my deluxe singlewide mobile home in the heart of Grayland Mobile Park."

"Mmm hmm, I like it."

He gave her a crooked, sexy smile and took a step closer, pinning her against the truck. Running his hands through her damp hair, he continued. "Then I was going to cook you some seafood and show off my culinary skills."

"Mmm hmm."

"And then I was going to take you on a date in town and maybe let you give me a hand job."

Willa snorted a laugh and smacked his arm. "Stop it, and be serious. My resolve is wavering."

The smile dipped from his face, and he leaned forward and kissed her forehead. "And then I was going to take you to meet my sister because I really like you, and I want Cassie to meet the woman who settles my bear."

Choked up, Willa cleared the thickness from her throat and tried to look severe. "No more girls."

"Only you."

"No more chasing tail and throwing attention at controlling skanks like Brittney."

He kissed her forehead again and whispered, "You have my word."

Hmm, the word of a playboy. "Matt, this is your warning. The second you mess up with another woman, you know I'm gone, right? That's not me, sticking around for a man who doesn't deserve my affection."

He smiled against her hairline and pulled her against him, more gently this time. "I wouldn't expect you to stick around for that bullshit. I won't mess this up."

She softened against him and wrapped her arms around his waist. With her head against his chest, she murmured, "Good. Now show me your trailer park."

SIX

"Whoa," Willa murmured, staring at the four trailers in a semi-circle just beyond the Grayland Mobile Park sign that stretched over the white gravel road. "This is not what I expected."

"What did you expect?" Matt asked from the passenger's seat. He had his elbow resting on the open window, and his eyes were lightened to that unsettling silver color as he watched her reaction. In his other hand was clutched the hideous salmon mug she'd gifted him.

"Trash in the yard and old ratty trailers and old cars with parts strewn everywhere." Instead, each trailer was uniform, covered in dark wood shingles like little mobile cabins. The roof on each looked new, and the white trim around the windows was crisp. The trailers each had a stone walkway that led to a huge communal fire pit in the middle. The grass around the community was neatly clipped, and each trailer had flowering landscaping on either side of the front door. The mountain scenery in the background was breathtaking. "Are these new homes?"

"Nah, they're thirty-five years old, but me and Creed cleaned them up when the Gray Backs first started recruiting new members."

She parked her truck behind Matt's Chevy that sat in front of the trailer at the end. A single pink, plastic flamingo had been stabbed into the immaculate side lawn. Nice.

"So you and Creed started this crew?"

"We did. We had to start our own because our bears...well, they're different and don't mesh that well with other shifters. We have to be picky about who we allow into the crew. Jason was next, then Clinton, then Easton. We stopped with him, though. Too many problem bears in one crew, and Creed couldn't handle any more dominant animals under him until we worked the kinks out. Which we never did. Five bears is all we can handle."

Five bears, and no room for mates. How was this supposed to work if they continued to date or mate or whatever it was bear shifters called what they were doing?

"The kids I grew up with were all different. Their animals weren't treated well, so it was always a struggle to make living together work."

"How old were you when you started taking care of them?"

"Sixteen. But really, it was before that. Sixteen was when I found us a safe place to live, though. Because of that, when it came time to make my own crew, I didn't mind accepting the problem shifters. Some of the Gray Backs would've been put down by other alphas by now, but they're safer with us, out here. Creed is dominant enough to manage us as long as we keep the numbers low."

Here was a man with a big heart who took risks for others. Who started a crew that no one else would fit into. When she was sixteen, she was worried about headgear, band competitions, and falling on her face in front of crushes she'd had in high school. Matt had been raising kids in the woods and working multiple jobs to feed and clothe them, sacrificing things she couldn't even imagine to make sure others were okay. He wasn't just the asshole woman-chaser that his social media pages showed. He was so much more.

She slid out of the truck and shut the door softly behind her.

Matt's fingers brushed her lower back as he guided her toward his trailer. Instead of the side entrance, he gently pushed her to a set of stairs that led to a screened-in porch facing the communal fire pit. From what she could see, all of the trailers boasted the porches. Cedar planks were sturdy under her feet, giving nary a creak as she stepped onto them. A rocking chair sat ready near a small table with an antique car magazine that was folded backward to show a picture of a refurbished Model T.

"Sorry," Matt muttered, hurrying around her to pick up the magazine.

She stared at him with a waiting grin. "You're a clean freak, aren't you?"

Matt frowned. "Maybe. My animal requires a decluttered den."

"That surprises me. In a good way. I expected empty pizza boxes and beer bottles everywhere."

"I recycle."

A snort blasted up her throat. "Have you ever brought a girl in here before?"

"To my den?" He looked baffled by her question. "No. Hell no. This place is...mine."

"Matt," she whispered, growing giddy. "Am I the first girl you brought into your den?"

"Of course." He said it like it should be obvious, but the only thing that was clear now was Matt was much more complicated than he let on.

He reached around her and opened the door that led inside. He came so close, his lips were only inches from hers. With a soft gasp, she froze, trapped in his gaze. His eyes dipped to her lips, and slowly, he leaned into her.

This wasn't a barely controlled passionate kiss like last night. This one was all soft lips and gentle sucks and sweet smacks as he pulled her closer. It was angled heads, soft brushes of his tongue, and fingertips in her hair.

This kiss wasn't desperate. It was a lovely peek into the part of Matt's heart that he hid from others.

As he eased away with a confused look in his sparking blue eyes, she murmured, "Remember that time you said you wouldn't ever sleep with a virgin?"

He nodded slowly.

"I think you'll have to get over that with me, Griz."

A faint smile curved his lips up. "Swear not

to laugh?"

"No."

"Gosh dangit, woman, why can't you just make something easy on me?" He inhaled deeply and played with a strand of her hair. "I'm nervous."

"About sleeping with me? We've both established this ain't your first rodeo, cowboy."

"Well, you saved yourself for a long time and—"

"I saved myself for the right person." She cupped his hands and pulled them to her cheeks just to feel his touch. "I saved myself for you. I want you to be my first, Matt."

"But what if I hurt you and you hate me and I lose you and I hate myself for the rest of my life—"

"And what if it's really special because you're gentle with me? At least for our first time."

He quirked one eyebrow and pulled her hand to his swim trunks. The long, thick roll of his erection was warm and hard against her hand.

"Holy cheeseballs," she murmured, looking down at his sizeable bulge in awe. "You're huge."

Matt chuckled. "Thanks, Nerd."

"No, I'm serious." She stood back and pressed the thin fabric on either side of his dick. The anatomy books in school did not look like Matt the Titan Dong. "Is it even physically possible for us to be together? I mean, I've touched myself plenty, and I'm a one finger kind of girl. Two just feels wild and crazy."

"Keep talking about touching yourself, and it'll only get bigger." His voice had gone deep and husky.

Reaching forward, she ran her palm up his length. His six-pack contracted, and he groaned softly, which drew a great big old grin from her face. His sensitivity to her touch was empowering. It was also warming her from the middle out.

"You smell like arousal," he murmured. The blue in his eyes transitioned to that beautiful silver color she was growing to adore. The color that said Matt was more than he seemed and his bear was close to the surface.

She brushed her fingertip just under his eye, then traced the long scars across his chest that ran parallel to his collarbone. The future was uncertain and full of questions, but here, in Matt's den, Willa was comfortable and safe.

Her every instinct said that Matt would protect her. He'd been searching for her, after all. *Her.* Not some perfect shell of a woman. Perfection hadn't settled his bear. She did. And as he looked at her with those mercury eyes, she felt like the luckiest person to have captured his attention.

Matt pushed the door open and picked her up.

"Are you carrying me over the threshold?" she asked.

"It feels right."

She slid her arms around his neck and cuddled against his strong torso as he kicked the door closed behind him. The screened-in porch led straight into his bedroom. It smelled like Matt and fabric softener, and one look at his dresser told her why. A hamper of neatly folded clothes sat atop it.

"I was going to put those away this morning, but I ran out of time."

It struck her as he set her gently on his bed how strong Matt was. He'd had barely any sleep last night because he'd taken it upon himself to drive her back to the camper and sleep beside her, and then he'd worked a physically grueling job, as well as sustained horrific injuries from something he hadn't been comfortable talking about. Even if his shifter healing was borderline magical, it still had to take its toll on him. Yet here he was, worrying over her opinion about his den and taking care of her comfort.

He knelt in front of her and slid her flip flops from her feet, then kissed her arches. "It'll be hard to keep my head when we're together," he admitted low. "Will you tell me if I hurt you?"

The insecurity in his eyes pulled at her heart. "I will."

His eyes pooled with some emotion she didn't understand. He looked away, so she pulled his gaze back to hers by cupping his cheek. "What is it?"

He leaned forward, brushed his lips against her knee before he answered. "This feels big."

"Are you scared?" she whispered.

He dipped his chin once and dragged his vulnerable eyes back to her.

Tears burned the backs of her eyes as he rested his cheek on her lap. Something in her, some instinct she couldn't ignore, told her Matt never admitted to fear, but he had with her. Protectiveness flooded her. "I'll take care of you," she promised.

"It's not that," he said on a breath.

"It feels like this is going to change something big in you?"

Another slight nod.

"Matt." She lifted his face from her lap with gentle fingers. "Maybe it's time for change."

"I know." He exhaled a shaky breath and stood, then padded toward the wall and flipped off the light switch.

Now, only the deep blue light of evening that filtered through the single window pane illuminated him on one side.

"What are you doing?" she asked.

"I always turn the lights off. It's more...comfortable."

"Because of your scars?"

"I guess."

"Turn them back on."

The click of the light was loud in the silence of his small room.

"I've seen your scars, and they only make me care about you more. You're more beautiful because of them."

A soft smile flickered across his face and disappeared again. "No one's ever called me beautiful before."

"No one knows you like me." Her heart sang that it was true. He'd grown too good at hiding, but now he was exposing his soft side for her alone. "I want to see you when you make love to me."

"Make love..." He blinked slowly as he approached. Kneeling in front of her again, he kissed her hand, then pulled her palm to a scar over his chest.

In this moment, Matt was easy to read. He had needs that ran as deep as canyons, but he hadn't dared to ask anyone before. And right now, he needed her touch to heal him, to show him he was accepted completely by her. Sniffling, she brushed her hand across the length of the slightly raised pink mark, then moved to the one below it. "Someday, you'll tell me what happened," she whispered as soft as a breath. "And I won't run. I'll care for you more because you let me in. Because I'll know you better."

His eyes didn't leave hers as she traced the map of his body. By the time she'd made her way to his abs, her breath trembled. She could almost feel the pain of his damaged nerve endings seeping through her touch. A tear fell down her cheek. She wished she could've shared this pain so it wouldn't have been so much on him.

"Shh." He wiped her damp cheek. "I'm okay

now."

Her fingers tingled with every scar she traced, as if she was drawing the heat into her, but she didn't want to stop. Brushing her lips against a mark that encircled the base of his neck, she pulled at the waist of his swim trunks until they slid down to his knees, then his ankles. Matt stepped out of them, and then pulled her cover-up over her head.

Now the nerves crept in. She was going to be bare before a man who had seen some of the most beautiful women on earth. What if she didn't measure up? She hesitated, her hands on the bottom of her tankini top.

"Come here," he said in a gentle tone. "I want to do that."

"Okay." She stood, unsteady on wobbly legs that didn't want to hold her anymore.

Matt pulled her tight against him, allowing his warmth to seep into her. And suddenly, she wanted to feel his skin against hers more than she'd ever wanted anything. Desire unfurled inside of her, spreading tendrils of aching want.

She closed her eyes as he pulled her swimsuit top over her head, unsure if she wanted to see his reaction. What if he was disappointed?

As if he could sense her reservation, he pulled her close again until their skin met. Her breasts pressed against the taut planes of his torso as he rubbed her back in gentle, rhythmic strokes.

"Your skin is so soft," he murmured in an awed voice.

Hugging his waist, she reveled in the feel of his chest against hers. She rubbed the uneven scars on his back, her fingers moving over them like waves. It was in this moment she realized something life altering. She'd never given much thought to love before, because she'd never felt anything so strongly in all her life, but Matt had pulled something from her she hadn't known she'd been harboring. She loved him. Loved how gentle he was with her. Loved how he let his guard down. Loved that he was sharing his skin—his secret self—with her.

Her heart pounded with the realization and, feeling brave, she eased back and pulled his hand to her chest. She wanted him to feel how much he affected her.

There was no hint of disappointment in his eyes as he raked his gaze down her body. With a steadying breath, she pushed down her shorts and swimsuit bottoms. "Be kind," she pleaded.

Matt turned and sat on the bed, holding her hips at an arm's length away as he studied her. His gaze had gone hungry and sent a shiver of anticipation up her spine.

"You're the most beautiful woman I've ever seen."

His voice rang with such honesty, her muscles relaxed and she slumped forward. "I was scared—"

"Don't," he said, eyes trapping her with that silvery glow. "Don't ever be afraid around me. You're perfect, Willa."

Running her hands through the sides of his hair, she stepped closer to him, settling in between his legs. With him sitting down, she was almost eye level with him. "You gonna kiss me or what?"

His response was instantaneous. Hand on her neck, thumb on her cheek, he leaned up, then sipped her lips with his. Her insides caught fire, and a helpless moan worked up her throat. Encased between his powerful legs, his hand so gentle on her face, Willa felt safe.

She'd been right to wait for Matt.

His jaw worked as he brushed his tongue against hers, and she smiled into the kiss. She would never get tired of this connection with him. Right on the verge of reading his thoughts, being able to finish his sentences, being on the exact same page with another living being—Matt had breathed new life into her.

Desperate to be closer, to feel the warmth pulsing from his skin, she straddled his lap, his erection pressed between her slowly soaking folds. Matt shuddered, his shoulders shaking with the remnants, and he pulled her harder against him, rolling his hips as he did.

His lips trailed down her jaw to her neck as he rocked against her again.

He was hitting right where she was most sensitive. It would be so easy to come like this. Damn, she was already close, but she wanted more. "Matt?"

A soft growl was the only answer.

"I did some research," she said breathily. "On Cora Wright's Web site, it said you don't get human sicknesses."

He nipped her collar bone and eased back to look at her, a slight frown marring his face. "No, I don't get sick. What are you really asking?"

"I'm on the pill."

He gripped her arms and searched her eyes, confusion swimming in the churning silver depths of his own. "I've always used a condom before."

"Good. I want to be the first you don't use one with."

His chest was heaving now as he shook his head slowly back and forth. "Willa, are you sure?"

She nodded and smiled. "I'm sure."

He spun her around and settled her back against the mattress, one hand strong on the leg she'd curled around his back. "Okay."

He reached between her legs and eased his finger inside of her, drawing another moan from her as his hand pressed softly against her clit. His finger made a wet sound as he pulled it out, and he smiled. "Who's sensitive now?"

Unable to answer, she bowed back against the comforter as he added a second finger and slid into her again, slower this time.

His breath hitched. "So wet," he murmured, pulling out of her.

The head of his cock brushed her, turning her insides to lava. Oh, he felt so good right there, barely in her. Rocking his hips, he pushed inside of her an inch, then eased out. Willa ran her hands down his flexed triceps. He was trying to keep his weight off her, sweet bear.

"Come here," she whispered.

Matt eased over her, up on his elbows now as he stroked her hair from her face. He kissed her slowly, tasting her, exploring her mouth as he pushed into her again, deeper this time. It burned and stretched.

"Relax your legs," he whispered against her lips.

Concentrating, she relaxed her muscles and pulled her leg up against his side, creating a better angle.

His abs flexed against her belly as he drove into her deeper, stretching her more. The small discomfort was nothing compared to the pleasure. His back flexed under her fingertips as he bucked into her slowly time and time again, deeper and deeper until he brushed her clit.

"Matt," she said on a sigh.

"Does it hurt too bad?" he asked.

"No. You feel good inside of me."

A breathtaking smile took his face as he wrapped his arm under her hips and pushed deeply into her again.

"Oooh," she drawled out, mesmerized at how something someone else was doing could feel so good.

He brushed his tongue against hers, his

muscles contracting each time he was buried deeply within her, as if his control was slipping.

"Willa," he rasped out, pumping into her faster. "God, I can't stop anymore. I can't—"

"Shh, then don't. I don't want you to. Ah!" She closed her eyes against the pressure building inside of her. The pleasure was so intense with each stroke, she couldn't form thoughts anymore. Couldn't do anything other than absorb each sensual blow.

Matt stroked into her faster and faster, holding her so tightly against him. A growl ripped through his chest and brought her closer to the edge.

Matt closed his eyes tightly, but opened them again, silver, churning, his animal right there, looking at her like she was everything good in his world. His breath shaking, muscles twitching, riding her harder, and she didn't care about the sting of pain in her middle. Not when it felt this good to be with him.

The growl settled in his chest, and he yelled out just as a pulsing orgasm exploded through her. A shot of wet heat filled her, and then another as Matt gritted out her name. She met his hips, crashing together as release filled them both.

Matt slowed, breathing hard, but his eyes on her—always on her. "Are you okay?"

Another aftershock pulsed through her, and she giggled, feeling high as a kite. "Better than okay." Was she sore? Yes, but that didn't take away from the beauty of this moment with the man she was falling hopelessly in love with.

She dragged kisses across a long scar near his collar bone, then nuzzled her face against him. "You did good, Griz. I knew you could be gentle."

Matt chuckled and eased out of her. A gush of warmth pulsed from between her legs.

"Shit," he said, startled. "You're bleeding. Not a lot, but I can smell iron."

She sat up as he looked down between them where they'd been connected. "Stay here." His voice had gone hard.

Had she done something wrong? Maybe she hadn't been as good at this as she'd felt a minute ago. Her confidence plunged as Matt disappeared into a small bathroom. The sound of the tap was loud in the sudden silence. It seemed to run forever before Matt turned it off and returned. He held a gray washrag, and when he pressed it between her legs, it was warm and comforting.

"I'm so sorry," he murmured in a broken voice.

"Hey." She cupped his cheek and pulled his attention to her. "I'm not sorry. That was always going to happen. Especially the first time."

His nostrils flared as he inhaled, then let out a long breath. "I thought I hurt you."

Stunned, she whispered, "I'm not a virgin anymore." A smile stretched her face. "It feels so weird. I've been waiting and wondering what it would be like for so long."

"And?" he asked, pulling the washrag gently across her sex again.

"And it was more amazing that I could've ever imagined."

Matt huffed a relieved sigh and kissed the nub of her oversensitive clit gently before he crawled up on the bed beside her. Curling his body around hers, he brushed his lips onto the back of her neck and said, "I'm glad you waited for me."

Willa smiled at the cream-colored wall of his room as happiness flooded her. Pulling at the edge of the comforter, she threw it over their legs and snuggled back against Matt. Her Matt.

All safe and warm and his, she whispered,

"Me, too."

SEVEN

"No!" Matt yelled, rocketing out of bed.

Willa's heart pounded against her ribcage as she sat straight up and squinted her eyes against the darkness. "What is it? Matt, what's wrong?"

He was crouched in the corner of his room, encased in shadows, the moonlight streaming through the window, illuminating his eyes and making them glow. His breath was loud, ragged, and the look on his face terrifying.

"It was a dream," he rasped out. "Only a dream. You're okay. Are you okay?"

"Yes, babe, come here. I'm okay."

Matt slunk to the bed, his gait uneven and hitched, as if his bear was still wary of danger. She pulled him down against her. "Tell me the dream."

"It doesn't matter."

"My mom always told me that when you have a bad dream, you should tell someone so it won't come true."

Matt's skin was clammy and cold under her hand, and she rubbed his back over and over to work warmth back into him.

He swallowed audibly in the dark. "You were in the Menagerie with me and Cassie, and Reynolds was taking you away to the tissue sample room."

"What's the Menagerie? And who is Reynolds?"

"And I was beating on the window, screaming for them to bring you back to me, but they dragged you into the room, and I couldn't see you anymore. And then I heard you screaming. Pain. I couldn't Change to save you. My sister and I beat on the window until our fists were bloody and the glass finally broke, but your screams had already died to nothing. I threw open the door, but it wasn't the tissue sample room anymore. It was woods. Piney woods. Hot. Sun shining through the canopy. And you were laying on this bloody, ripped up mattress, and I thought you were dead. So much blood. But you opened your eyes and...and..."

"Finish it fast," she said, so scared she

couldn't move.

"And your eyes were silver, like mine."

"It was just a dream, Matt. Only a dream," she chanted to calm him as much as herself. She'd had nightmares before, but never about someone she cared about being hurt. "What's the Menagerie?" she asked again, quieter this time.

"Don't want to talk no more," he said in a gravelly deep voice she didn't recognize. His eyes blazed in the moonlight as he pulled her ankles to the end of the bed.

"Okay," she whispered, spreading her bare legs. "Do you need me?"

"Too soon. You'll hurt." His fingers were frantic as he worked the panties she'd put on after dinner down her legs.

"Then what do you—" Oooh.

He plunged his tongue into her, lapping, his fingers digging into her hips as she arched back against the bed. She gripped his hair when he slowed down and rolled her hips with each stroke. Easing out of her, he sucked gently on her clit. A soft growl rattled between her legs, and she cried out his name at how good it felt. Tongue in her again, Matt gripped her ass and pulled her closer.

This time, she wasn't sore at all. There was

no pinch of pain, no reservation. Only pleasure. Matt ate her as if he'd known her body for years. Kissing, thrusting, drawing her closer to orgasm with every deep, lapping lick.

"Oh my gosh," she cried out, louder than she'd intended, but fuck it all, this was awesome. Release pounded through her, and before her aftershocks were even done, he leapt up on the bed and straddled her hips, stroking his long shaft hard and fast.

Desperate to feel his completion in some form, she pulled her sleepshirt over her head just as he leaned forward on the balls of his feet and groaned. Hot, creamy jets shot from the swollen head of his cock, and she gripped his tensed legs as he showered her breasts and stomach. Holy shit, this was hot—sexy Matt, coming on her skin like he was marking his territory.

Warmth wept down her ribs and onto the comforter, but she didn't care about keeping his bed clean. She cared that his muscles were relaxing and the effects of that awful nightmare were being washed away from him.

With a groan, he lay down beside her and cuddled her close. He released a sigh against her hair and trailed his fingers up and down the curve of her waist. Her sexy bear shifter, taken with lust for her, but caring enough to make sure she knew she was adored afterward.

Willa hugged him tight and pressed her knee in between his, thankful he was okay.

"Sleep," he urged. "I won't let anything happen to you."

The last words he'd spoken like a promise to himself.

EIGHT

His mate was a sound sleeper. The smell of bacon and the sound of the sizzling skillet hadn't woken her, and the glass he'd dropped on the counter and nearly broken hadn't stirred her either.

A wave of cocky pride washed over him, and he allowed a private smile. Hell yeah, she was sleeping like a stone. He'd rocked her world last night. No. He frowned down at the orange juice he was pouring. Last night hadn't been like anything he'd done with any other girl. It wasn't some wild night for the brag book. Sex with Willa had changed everything.

Last night was the first time his bear had ever gotten the urge to claim a woman. He'd have to keep sex with her to missionary position since going at her from behind was going to make it really hard for him not to sink his teeth into her neck and Turn her. She was his mate. Had been since the first time he'd seen her, but Willa was human and was going to stay that way.

If he told her how devoted he was to her already, it would scare her. Hell, it scared him.

All right—bacon, eggs, toast with a little bowl of strawberry jam, and orange juice. This was the first time he'd ever made a woman breakfast in bed, and once again, as he often was around Willa, he found himself nervous. Her opinion meant the world. More than Kong's or Creed's or Cassie's even.

Willa didn't know it yet, but she toted the power to destroy him.

He padded into his bedroom with the tray of breakfast. He wore only a pair of low slung sweat pants. For the first time ever, he didn't care that his scars were on display in front of a woman. She'd seemed disappointed when he'd put on a shirt to sleep in last night when they'd crawled into bed together, so he'd pulled it off and let her run her fingers absently over his uneven skin as she drifted off to sleep.

When he saw her face in the early morning light, he stopped short, almost toppling the glass of juice. A couple of strands of her bright red hair had fallen over her face as she hugged the pillow next to her, but not even that could hide how beautiful she was.

He smiled at her death grip on the pillow. She was a cuddler. He'd learned that last night when she moved with him every time he rolled over or moved his leg. He was usually restless in his sleep, but last night hadn't been so bad. She chased away his ghosts, and after the nightmare, she'd given him peace.

He wasn't into cuddling in general, but it was different with Willa. Holding her settled his restless animal.

Outside, Creed whistled an ear-splitting sound. Ten minutes until it was time to load into their trucks and head up the mountain road to the new jobsite the big boss-man, Damon Daye, had assigned them.

God, he was going to miss Willa.

Creed gave a second whistle. That one was for Clinton, who never woke up on time.

Willa opened her eyes a crack and stretched with the cutest fucking squeak he'd ever heard.

"I made you breakfast." It was the least he could do after coming to her needy and barely in control after that nightmare.

Willa sat up, hair ruffled with a big old grin stretching her face. "That's the nicest thing anyone has ever done for me. I feel like I'm in a romantic movie."

He chuckled and set the tray on the table. He was pretty sure no one would ever make a movie that involved bear shifters.

"How long do you have before work?" she asked.

"Creed just gave the ten minute warning. I don't want to leave you, but we have to make up for bad timber numbers yesterday. Easton picked a fight and cut our day short."

"Is that why you were all torn up when I met you at the falls yesterday?"

"Yeah. It's Gray Back tradition."

"What is?"

"To fight like hell and make everything more difficult than it has to be."

She laughed, but she wouldn't if she knew how serious he was being. Gray Backs probably bled more than any other crew.

"Okay, give me a minute." Willa slid off the bed and jogged for the bathroom.

She beamed at him just before she closed the door. What was she doing?

The tap turned on, and he could hear the rhythmic brushing of her teeth. "Your juice is going to taste nasty now," he called through the door.

By the time she finished in the bathroom, he had about five minutes before Creed came busting down his door.

She threw open the bathroom door and ran for him, then leapt into his arms with a giggle. Knuckles on her forehead, she arched back and said, "Take me, sexy grizzly man."

"Take you? Woman, I have five minutes max, and I imagine you're sore as hell this morning. Bad idea."

"Or awesome idea. Five minute challenge. Stop telling me no." She pulled at the elastic waist of his sweats. "This is going to happen. I will be driving all over creation today trying to keep busy while you work, and this has to tide me over until I get to see you again. And besides, I'm not that sore. Come on, man. You're wasting seconds."

With a growl, he gave in and laid her on the edge of the bed, then tore through her panties with a satisfying *riiip*.

"Matt! Those are my favorite—"

He kissed her hard, swallowing the rest of her complaint. She tasted like Willa and cool mint, and when that sexy moan she did so well sounded, he plunged his finger into her to make sure she was ready. She was. His mate got wet on a dime for him, and pride surged through him that he'd found someone so perfect for him. God, he was hard. Harder than hard, he was already throbbing, as if he was ready to come just thinking about her wet pussy.

He slid into her halfway. Damn, she was tight. Tight and wet and perfect. Easing out, he reveled in the little pleading sound she gave him. Fuck, he couldn't get enough of her. He slid into her until she gasped when he hit her just right. Another stroke, and he was losing control. Bear snarling through him, he bucked into her again. Trying to keep from hurting her, he gripped the comforter and set his teeth against her neck, grazing her but not biting down. Never biting down. He wouldn't Turn her. Wouldn't ruin Willa's life.

"Do it," she said.

"What?"

"Bite me." Her voice came out desperate, husky as her hips moved against his.

"You don't know what that means."

"I do so. Claim me."

Shit. Focus. So close. Gonna blow...

He slammed into her faster, and she met him stroke for stroke. He could hear them now, skin slapping together, the slick sound of his dick sliding in and out of her. So tight. All of his nerve endings were having a fucking holiday. God, oh God.

"Fuck," he gritted out as he blew his load into her.

She yelled as she clamped down around him in quick pulses. Yes, that was his girl. Coming for him fast and hard. His hips jerked as he shot into her a few more times, emptying himself completely.

"Let's load up!" Creed yelled outside.

Matt kissed Willa, lapping his tongue against hers just to taste his mate. Her eyes had gone hazy. "Stay as long as you want." *Stay your whole life if you want.* "I have to go. I'll be home around seven if you want to come back here. Or I can meet you in town."

"Here. I'll meet you here," she murmured in a dreamy voice.

He nibbled her lip and slid out of her slowly. There was that scent of iron in the air again. She was bleeding. He couldn't wait until she was totally healed and could take his size without pain or damage. That right there was a big part of the reason he hadn't ever slept with a virgin. But Willa wasn't just any virgin. She was his. His Willa, his woman, his mate.

Matt dressed in a rush, conscious of her eyes on him the entire time. He kissed her quick, and said, "I can't wait to see you tonight," then ran for the door. He threw it open just as Creed was jogging up his porch steps looking pissed.

"I'm coming."

"From what I heard, you already came. What the fuck did I tell you about potential mates in the trailer park, Barns?"

Okay, Creed was irate. As he should be. There was no more denying Willa was a potential mate. She was the one. Fuck, Creed was going to hurt him today.

"Ream me out on the landing. I don't want Willa to hear," he pleaded low.

"I'm not going to ream you out, Barns. I'm going to bleed you for disobeying my orders." Creed spun around and strode for his truck where Clinton was hanging out the window pointing and silently laughing, the prick.

"Get the fuck out of my ride," Creed yelled at Clinton. "Go ride with Easton."

"Aw, man," Clinton said. "I don't want to ride with Easton. He's weird and will probably drive us off a cliff just for funsies."

Creed stopped in his tracks. "Why does everyone think that whatever I say is a suggestion? That's a fuckin' order, Clinton. I swear to God..." Creed kept muttering, but

Matt couldn't hear what he was saying under his breath anymore as he stomped around the back of his truck. "Get in, Matt!"

"This is your fault," Clinton said, kicking a rock as he sauntered toward Easton's truck.

Easton stood leaned against his old beat-up Ford, green eyes dancing as he gave Clinton a predatory grin.

Aw, shit, Matt did feel bad now. Today was going to suck for everyone. Everyone except Jason, who had the day off and was enjoying the show from his front porch with a big old grin on his face as he blew on a mug cupped in his hands. He was also incredibly naked, as he always enjoyed his coffee in the mornings, dick out for all to see.

Fuck it all, Creed was right. A woman didn't belong up here.

His inner bear snarled his disagreement.

Sack lunch in hand, Matt slid into the passenger's seat of Creed's truck and slammed the door beside him.

"You need to cut that snarly shit out, Matt."

Matt swallowed hard and forced the sound in his throat to stop.

Creed jammed the key, and the engine roared to life. "Who is she?"

"You met her yesterday. Her name's

Willamena Madden. She just graduated college, and she's here on vacation."

"No, dipshit. Who is she to you?"

The truck lurched forward as Creed slammed his foot on the gas.

Matt rolled down the window to ease the electricity that snapped from Creed's skin toward him. His alpha's bear was a gnarly beast to mess with, and Matt was practically pulling the damned thing's stump tail just by breathing right now.

"She's the one."

Creed shot him a look. Eyes round, mouth hanging open—that kind of look. Matt's lip lifted in a snarl, and he looked out through the woods that were passing in a blur.

"Have you lost your mind? She's human, Matt. I've already forbade you all from Turning anyone, and there's a reason for that."

"I'm not Turning her, Creed. I wouldn't do that to her."

"Then what's the plan, man? Cause I have to tell you, I don't see this working out for any of us."

"The Ashe Crew has human mates—"

"The Ashe Crew is the A team, Matt! We're the fucking C team. You know why? Because our dumbasses went and recruited all the problem bears."

"For a reason."

"Doesn't matter what our reasons were, Matt. The only way this works is if we don't complicate our lives up here. Women complicate things. Mates complicate things. Humans complicate things. Willamena Madden is a fucking time bomb." Creed ran his hand roughly over his black hair and spat out the open window. "She can't stay here. I'm not going back on my orders."

"Her place is with me if she wants it."

"Yeah? And what am I supposed to do with that? Can you even imagine Clinton or Jason thinking 'Aw, Matt found a mate. That looks fun. I think I'll go find one?' What about Easton? Do you want to unleash Easton on Saratoga looking for a woman to bring back to the trailer park because you have someone to fuck, and he wants that, too? Our crew would singlehandedly traumatize all the women within a hundred mile radius. It's not just fun and games, Matt. Not when we have bears like him to manage."

"Creed, stop. Willa's here for a week on vacation. I don't even know if she'll stay for me. You could be freaking out over nothing."

Creed's voice went hard as steel and

deadly low. "Or it could be the worst thing to ever happen to our crew."

"Yeah, well what do you want me to do? I've been searching for a mate for years, and she's finally found me. I'm finally feeling in control of my future, and one of my best friends is giving me shit over it. You could've said 'Congrats man, I know you've been through hell, and you deserve some peace.' You could've! Instead, you're up my ass about how I've ruined everyone's life by finding someone who can settle me. I love her, Creed. I fucking love her. Let that sink in. I actually have enough feeling left in me after all the shit I went through to love something."

Creed slammed his hand against the steering wheel and let out a string of cuss words Matt had never heard put together before.

Let his alpha curse his name. It didn't change the way Matt felt about Willa.

Creed turned onto a switchback and accelerated on the straightaway. They'd be at the landing soon, and his alpha had stopped talking completely. Instead, he seemed lost in thought as he rubbed his two day stubble absently. "What am I supposed to do here, Matt?" It was the first time Creed had sounded uncertain since he'd claimed his alpha rank over the Gray Backs.

Matt sighed miserably. He didn't want to stress out his friend, his alpha. "Can we see how the boys are around Willa? Let her hang out this week and see if they can treat her right? See if they can control their bears around her? If they can't, I'll leave. I'll move wherever she is and try to make it work."

"No, Matt," Creed said in a hoarse voice. "You're a Gray Back. I don't want you to go."

"Then let's hope the boys are okay with her because I can't live where she isn't allowed."

Creed scratched his head and muttered one last curse. "Okay. We'll see how the boys are with her." He pulled to a stop near the landing and leveled him with a look. "I sure hope your mate is strong enough to handle them."

His alpha got out of the truck and slammed the door behind him. Pain stabbed through Matt just thinking about leaving his life here. Leaving his people.

He too hoped with everything in him that Willa was strong enough to handle the Gray Backs.

NINE

When Willa's phone chirped, she pulled it from her purse and stared down at the screen. She'd just received a text message from *Griz*. Ha. When had Matt put his number in her phone?

I'm sorry if you saw Jason's dick this morning.

She laughed too loud and the woman next to her at the Hobo Hot Pool jumped. With a glare, she glided farther away through the steaming water.

"Sorry," Willa murmured.

She had actually seen Jason's swinging dick this morning when she'd packed up the Tacoma to head into town for the day. He'd stood splay-legged on his porch, hands on his hips and neck arched back like he was enjoying the sunlight on his bare skin. "Lovely day," he'd said in a conversational tone.

Willa's eyes had just about bugged out of her head, and she'd nearly choked on the last piece of bacon she'd been chewing on. "What are you doing?" she'd asked, trying to look everywhere but between his legs.

"It's a morning ritual."

"All right then. Well, you and your...ritual...have a nice day," she'd said before she drove off.

Do all werebears have giant dicks? she typed out, then hit send.

Do you have a problem with nudity? Modesty doesn't exist with the Gray Backs. Will that make you uncomfortable? Or is it something you think you can handle?

Willa slipped back into the natural hot spring pool and leaned on the edge, staring at her phone. Matt's question seemed uncharacteristically serious.

Is this a test? she typed out.

Kind of. Creed said you could hang out at Grayland on a trial basis.

So he lifted the rules? I can stay nights with you while I'm here?

Yeah. Got to go. Lunch break is done. Crawfish boil tonight. Will u come?

What time?

Seven

I'll see you then

Another text came through. *This morning was fun*

A grin cracked her face as she responded. *For me too, you sexy bear. I like your big 8---D*

Moments ticked by before Matt's response made her phone chirp again. *Good, cause I love your (0)*

She laughed too loud again, but this time, she didn't care. Last night wasn't a one night stand. She'd known in her heart it wasn't, but her head was still stuck on Matt being a playboy. But he'd gotten his alpha to lift the rules they'd broken last night, and now she was being invited back because of Matt.

Pressure suddenly pushed against her chest and made it hard to breathe. He'd said this was kind of a test. Creed's test? Matt's test? It felt important that she make a good impression with his friends. Now more than ever, it became apparent just how much pull Creed had with his crew. He could kick her out of Matt's life for good.

Crap.

Willa climbed out of the Hobo Hot Pool and tiptoed across the pavement to her bag. Toweling off, she began ticking off the ingredients she'd need from the grocery store.

Mom had always said the way to a man's heart was through his belly.

Willa had the beginnings of a plan and grandma's recipe memorized.

She sure hoped Creed liked homemade gumbo with his crawfish.

****

Jason was squatting down by a gargantuan silver pot when Willa pulled into the Grayland Mobile Park. He nodded his chin in greeting, his dark eyes focused on his task at hand, which, at the moment, seemed to be adjusting a propane tank and lighting a burner under the pot.

"Back so soon? You must be aching for some trouble."

"Or I am the trouble," she teased, pulling the first paper grocery bag from the back seat.

Jason snorted. "Sounds about right. What do you have there?"

"I'm making gumbo tonight."

Jason stood. He still didn't have a shirt on, but at least now he was wearing pants. "From scratch?" The surprise in his voice was borderline offensive.

"Yep." She hefted another bag to her hip.

"You a Louisiana girl by any chance?"

"I grew up in Minden. How'd you guess?"

"The accent sounded familiar." Jason thumped his chest. "I'm from just outside of New Orleans. A bayou bear, Turned and raised."

"Really? Is that why they put you in charge of the crawfish?"

"Ha, no. Your boy is controlling about the crawfish. I'm the potato and onions guy, and sometimes I add the corn if he's feeling generous."

"Matt cooks?"

"Matt controls. He can't help himself. His bear is...well...you know."

She didn't know, but maybe Matt should tell her if he had problems with his animal. "You said you were Turned?"

"Yep, right after my twenty-first birthday."

Willa struggled with full arms to a prep table where Jason had obviously been shucking corn cobs.

"Who Turned you?"

Jason's smile faded from his lips as he pulled the lid off the pot with what looked like a metal paddle. "My mate."

"Oh." Obviously he wasn't paired up anymore, and his shuttered eyes said he didn't want to talk about it, so she didn't push.

They worked in silence after that, but it wasn't awkward. It was the comfortable kind where they didn't have to use small talk to fill a void. They worked side-by-side on the prep table, and he even offered to show her how to turn on the brick outdoor stove. And when he'd done that, he jogged into Matt's trailer and came back with a large boiling pot for her to start making a roux.

Now, she liked to do her roux low and slow, so she was barely done with it by the time Jason said, "Look like you're workin'. Boss and them boys are headed back, and Creed is in a foul mood today. He just about ripped my ear off through the phone earlier when he told me to get the crawfish."

"Because of me?"

"Yep."

"Shit, Jason, you could've sugarcoated it a little bit."

"No sugar around here, trouble. Only spice."

Minutes later, she heard what must've warned Jason of his crew's imminent arrival. Rumbling trucks and creaky brakes. Nervous flutters filled her stomach thinking about Creed's anger. She hated being the cause of a rift in the Gray Back Crew.

She scooped her chopped holy trinity—bell peppers, onions, and celery—into the dark roux, and stirred them constantly as the roar of engines grew closer and closer.

Her palms were sweating now, and as much as she wished she could blame it on working around high heat, she was nervous from her hairline to her toes. By the time the two trucks pulled down the main, white gravel road that curved through the trailer park, her hands were shaking something fierce.

A tall man with sandy brown hair and striking green eyes was out of a jacked-up old white Ford first. The slamming door echoed through the mountains. He cast one angry look at her, and she gasped. Blood ran from his ear, down the side of his neck, and he was carrying his arm strangely. It hung limply at his side, and crimson dripped off his middle finger in a constant *pit, pat, pit, pat.*

"What happened?"

The anger in the man's face faltered. "I'm Easton." His voice was too gravelly to be completely human, and his eyes were glowing that odd green color.

"I'm Willa. Are you okay?"

He looked down at his arm, then slid a confused look at her. "I'm fine." Easton turned and strode up a worn trail that led into the thick pine woods.

A traumatized-looking Clinton stepped out of the other side of Easton's truck. "You sure as hell know how to make an entrance."

"Wait, I do?" She looked at Matt and Creed, who were getting out of the alpha's truck more slowly, then back at Clinton. "What do you mean?"

"You spent one night here, and the Gray Backs are already bleeding for you."

"Okay," she drawled, a snap of anger blasting through her. "That's bullshit. Y'all bleed all the time because you won't stop fighting. Don't pretend that crap started happening the second I showed up."

Clinton's blond brows arched high, and a slow smile split his face. "You aren't going to take my shit, are you?"

"Not yours. Your alpha's, though? Yes. Matt told me Creed is the boss man. You're just a peon like me," she said to Clinton with a wink.

"Shit, girl, I like you already. What smells good?"

"Gumbo," she called over her shoulder as she scooped andouille sausage into the pot.

Matt's hands slid around her middle, and he rested his forehead on her shoulder from behind.

"You hurt?" she asked quietly.

"It's nothing that won't heal."

With a sigh, she turned and tried to control her fear when his eyes were that unexpected blazing silver color.

A soft growl rattled his throat. "Don't like when you smell scared."

"Let me see."

"Willa," he said with a slow shake of his head.

"Hurry up before I burn my roux."

Matt slid his inhuman eyes to the steaming pot, then lifted his shirt. Four perfect slices curved around his ribcage, probably created from Easton's claws. Already, they were half-healed, but the bottom cut, the deepest, was still weeping red, and his white T-shirt looked like a crime scene.

"Geez, Matt," she murmured. "Does it hurt bad?"

He nodded his chin once. "I need a minute." He took off toward his trailer with long strides.

"What about the crawfish?" Jason asked. "They're ready to go in."

"You do it."

Jason gave Willa a look that said he was

shocked to his bones, and then a slow grin stretched his face. "Well, that's a first. Maybe having you around to settle his bear won't be so bad after all."

Giddy and humming, Jason pulled the bag of live crawfish from the shady patch under the prep table and pulled a knife from his back pocket. Willa added some turkey sausage and chicken stock and kept a constant stir as she watched Jason dump the mud bugs into a holey bucket and run a hose over them.

Creed pulled a plastic chair up next to the stove and handed her an already opened bottle of beer. "You cooking to win my favor?"

"Shit yeah," she muttered. The swig of cold beer tasted like heaven as it slid down her throat. "You make me nervous."

"You didn't look scared of blood when Matt showed you his ribs, so that's one point in your favor. What all do you know about us?"

"Just what Matt's told me and what I read on Cora Wright's Web site. She was the one in charge of helping the Breck Crew come out to the public. She does question and answer forums and has a bunch of frequently asked questions on her site."

"I know who Cora is. She advised us when we registered to the public, too."

"Oh, right. Of course. Sorry."

Creed took a long drink of his beer and stared thoughtfully at Jason, who was dumping a heap of pre-mixed, seasoning into the boiling pot. It was spicy enough to burn her nose from ten feet away.

"You know about claiming?" Creed asked.

The nerves were back, and if she answered him now, her voice would shake. She busied herself with tossing grandma's secret seasoning ingredients into the gumbo. Finally, after she'd added chicken breast and okra, she answered him. "I do. At least, I think I do. Cora Wright's—"

"Web site told you."

"Yeah." Heat blasted up her neck and into her cheeks as she thought about how she'd asked Matt to bite her. She'd lost her damned mind in the throes of passion with him because she didn't really want to be Turned into a bear shifter. She was perfectly happy with her human status.

"What are your intentions with Matt?" Creed asked low. "I need to know. Whatever is happening between you puts my crew at risk, and I need to know you feel the same about him as he feels about you."

"I miss him when he's away from me. I feel

like he gets me like no one ever has, which I realize makes no sense because we haven't known each other that long. But that doesn't seem to matter to my silly heart because I feel like I've known him all my life. I breathe for his smile, and when he's hurting, I hurt. And when I touch his scars..." This was too much. She was sharing things with Creed she hadn't meant to, but he'd asked her a direct question, and it was as if she'd taken some sort of truth serum. Maybe Creed was magic. She believed in it.

"Look," she said, pulling the spoon from the pot and looking the alpha right in the eyes. "I'm falling in love with him. I don't know what tomorrow will bring, or next week. And as much as I've tried to convince myself this is some vacation fling, I know it's not. Matt feels...important."

"And you don't care about all those other women?"

"I wish he hadn't been with them. I wish I had all of his firsts to myself, but that was in his past, and I trust him. I don't care about where he's been. I care about where he's going."

Creed huffed a heavy sigh and lifted his beer. He tapped the neck against hers with a soft *clink*, then said, "All right, we'll try this. You can stay here until my crew proves to me they can't handle having a woman up here."

"And if they can handle it?"

"You can stay the whole week."

A week. She turned back to the pot and began stirring it again. Creed had just reminded her that she was a temporary fixture here at the trailer park. Logically, she'd known that. She was here on vacation, nothing more. But suddenly this trip-gone-wrong and the fallout with the bombshells felt big. It felt like fate. This place with Matt was comfortable in ways she'd never expected.

One week, and she'd go back to her life in Minden.

One week, and she'd have to say goodbye to Matt and the people here.

One week was all she had to make memories that would last her whole life.

TEN

"Clinton, quit!" Willa yelled, trying not to laugh as she pulled a third crawfish out from under her shirt.

Clinton was chortling like a lunatic as he danced out of swatting range.

"See," Matt called from the road where he and Jason were tossing a football to each other from a ridiculously long distance apart. "This is why I don't trust them to cook. Food wasters, all of them. Leave her alone, or I'll eat you."

"From what we heard all night, you should be full of eating people," Clinton said.

Willa's eyes nearly popped out of her head as she scooped rice into paper bowls. "Clinton!"

"The walls are thin. Oh, Matt. Oh!" he crowed in a high-pitched voice.

Mortified, Willa hid her searing face and scooped gumbo into each bowl.

"Where's Easton?" she asked, desperate to change the subject.

Creed leaned back on the prep table and jerked his chin to the woods. "At his place."

One, two, three, four. How had she not realized there were only four trailers in the semi-circle and five bears in the Gray Back Crew?

"Why does he live up there?"

"Uh, because when he moved here two years ago, Matt pissed him off day one, and Easton picked his trailer up and dragged it through the woods," Clinton explained helpfully.

"Picked it up and dragged it through—you mean with his bare hands?"

"Easton needs to live in confinement. His bear does best away from the rest of us," Creed said as he lifted the draining pot of crawfish out of the water and settled it on the top ledge.

"That's sad," she said, heart aching at what could make a man need such solitude.

"Spare your pity for someone who deserves it," Matt muttered as he approached the fire pit, tossing the football up and catching it. "Beaston lives the way he lives because he chooses to."

Clinton snorted and repeated, "Beaston."

Beaston? Willa tossed a look at the trail he'd walked up earlier. She should be afraid of all these men, but for some reason, she wasn't. Perhaps her instincts were broken.

"Food's on," Matt said, pouring the crawfish, corn, potato and onion boil onto thick brown paper Creed has spread over the prep table.

"Shouldn't we tell Easton?" she asked as everyone gathered around and began twisting tails off the steaming crawfish.

"You can try, but it'll be a waste of breath," Jason said around a bite. "He doesn't like social calls."

Well, she knew exactly how it felt to be left out by the bombshells, and she'd be damned if she was going to do that to someone else.

After Creed dug into his bowl of gumbo, he rolled his eyes heavenward. "Damn, woman, you can cook."

She grinned and thanked him, then snatched a bowl of the piping food and headed for the trail that led to Easton's wilderness trailer.

"Willa," Matt warned.

"I'm not leaving him out."

She could feel Matt's eyes boring into the back of her head, but she was doing this. The evening had been perfect, and she was enjoying getting to know Matt's crew, but there was something seriously disjointed when one of them was so ostracized like this.

She stomped up the uneven trail, clutching her warm bowl of gumbo, but with every step farther into the woods, her confidence wavered.

The boys called him Beaston for a reason, and here she was, like a horror-movie dumbass, headed out to his hidey hole alone, all human and weaponless.

But if she was really in danger, Matt wouldn't have let her come out here by herself.

Easton's trailer sat in a small clearing. A large woodpile covered most of the front of the house, but why he was stockpiling wood like this when it was summertime, she hadn't a guess. Perhaps he needed to chop it to settle his animal? Her hands shook even more.

"Easton?" She didn't lift her voice too loudly. He was a bear shifter and would hear her. Hell, he probably heard her tromping through the woods like a tranquilized elephant. She wasn't graceful, or even quiet, when she walked.

The door banged open and Easton stuck his head out, green eyes narrowed on her, then on the bowl in her hands.

"I come in peace," she joked with a little snort.

He didn't smile.

Scrunching up her nose to readjust her glasses, she walked carefully up his porch stairs and handed him the bowl. "I made gumbo. We're all eating if you want to join us."

Easton frowned, eyes still on the bowl. "You want me to eat with you?"

"With all of us, yeah."

"I hurt your mate."

Mate. That word sent chills skittering up her spine. "He hurt you back." She gestured at his arm, which he seemed to be able to use now.

His unsettling gaze drifted to his arm, then back to her. So fast he blurred, he snatched the bowl from her hands and disappeared inside.

Okaaay. She turned to leave, but her name whispered softly froze her in her tracks.

"A gift for a gift," Easton said gruffly behind her.

On his palm was a hunting knife, encased

in fine leather. Willa swallowed hard and took the knife, then unsheathed it slowly. The silver glistened in the evening sunlight, and the blade looked sharp as a razor. "It's beautiful. Did you make this?"

Easton nodded once.

"Thank you." She shifted her weight from side to side.

He was watching her now with an unreadable expression.

Clearing her throat nervously, she said, "There's plenty of food down there."

Easton shook his head and turned, then disappeared inside his trailer, the door banging loudly behind him.

Clutching her knife, Willa made her way back down the trail. Easton might be more bear than man, but he'd given her a present when she'd shown him kindness. Wild as he might be, he still had good in him.

"Told you," Jason said when she returned and settled into an opening by Matt's side. "And here I thought you were intelligent."

Willa tucked Easton's gift in her back pocket and plucked her first crawfish from the enormous pile of food. Twisting the tail, she exposed the seasoned meat inside. "Why do you think that?"

"Because you wear glasses and talk fancy. I bet you even went to college."

"You'd win that bet," she said. She gripped the spicy meat in her teeth and pinched the tail to release it from the hard shell. Oh damn, this was good. Whatever spicy seasoning Jason had used was perfect.

"I bet you majored in something super nerdy," Jason said, licking his fingers.

"I did. I majored in micro-penises, and you have the perfect specimen."

Matt snorted beside her, and Clinton slapped Jason on the back as he let off a booming laugh. Even Creed was hiding a smile from the end of the table.

She shoved her glasses farther up her nose with her shoulder as the sound of eating and joking hummed around her. This reminded her of crawfish boils she'd had at family reunions when she was growing up. Back when Grandma and Mom were still around. She and Dad had never picked up the tradition after they passed, and now she regretted that. Maybe dinners like this could've fixed what was missing with her and Dad.

Movement along the tree line grabbed her attention, and the others looked up in unison, as if instinct had drawn their gazes. Easton paced just inside of the shadows.

"Well, come on," Creed called out, waving his hand. "Food won't last forever."

"I'll be damned," Jason murmured as Easton made his way around the trucks and toward the table.

He didn't join them right away. Instead, he grabbed another bowl of rice and gumbo before he came to stand beside Clinton.

"Food's good," Easton muttered with a quick look at her. "I forgot to say thank you."

"The knife was thanks enough." Willa was getting all choked up with happiness that he had joined them.

"You got a knife?" Clinton asked. "I've been asking for one of Easton's knives for two years." Turning to Easton, he said, "Why does she get one?"

Easton frowned and scooped another bite into his maw. Gulping it down, he growled out, "Because I like her, and you're an asshole."

"Oh," Clinton muttered before he went back to peeling crawfish. "Fair enough."

Matt chuckled warmly beside her and pulled her snug against his side. He'd been quiet tonight, but she couldn't tell if it was because his injury was still hurting or if he was exhausted from work or what. All she knew was that she was happy his distance didn't seem to be caused by something she'd done.

And as she looked around the table, a warm, fuzzy sensation filled her middle. Jason and Clinton were tossing empty crawfish shells at each other, while Creed shook his head and laughed. Easton ate her gumbo stoically, and Matt—her Matt—whispered in her ear. "I missed you today."

Moments like these were ones she'd remember all her life. Tonight, she felt like she belonged, and that was a rare thing. She'd drifted from the bombshells to other friends she kept at a distance, just so she wouldn't get hurt again. And she'd been stung when she'd tried to reconnect with Brittney, Kara, and Gia on this trip, but here, things were different.

She didn't feel like an outcast with this crew. She wasn't the ugly friend or the wingman. She wasn't the pity call or the tagalong.

She was just Willa—knife-wielder, good cook, easy banterer, smarty-pants, lover-of-fun, and potential mate of Matt Barns.

She hadn't ever fit into a box, but here, no one tried to shove her into one.

In the Grayland Mobile Park with these off-kilter bear shifters, she could be herself, and it was enough.

ELEVEN

Bear Trap Falls, six thirty, don't bring clothes.

Matt's texts were never dull. Skinny dipping? Okay, she'd never done that, but she was game.

Willa pulled her Tacoma up to the clearing near the river an hour early, then saddled herself down with a bag chair, cooler of fruity beer, and a beach towel. Just the thought of relaxing on the shore was enough to push away the stress of the week coming to an end. Tomorrow, she was supposed to pack up her camper and head back home. The bombshells had already left, citing that Saratoga was too boring for them. Willa had tried not to giggle when Kara had called her and told her that.

Saratoga had turned out to be the least boring place she'd ever been.

Her days had been filled with exploring the growing list of local attractions that Matt compiled for her, and her evenings had been spent with the Gray Backs. This week, she'd learned how to drive an ATV through mud, fish for trout, and climb trees. The last bit was because Clinton had hung out with her on his day off and dared her to hang a rope swing from one of the old trees near the river. She'd hung that thing like a boss, then giggled herself breathless when Matt had nearly fileted Clinton for putting her at risk. Protective, sexy bear.

And nights...oh, nights in Matt's trailer were magic. She'd learned lots and lots of interesting lessons from him this week.

She set up her chair and pulled a book from her bag. Clad in the tiny green triangle bikini she'd bought earlier this week and a floppy hat, she settled in the sun for an hour with her guilty pleasure. She'd read three saucy romances this week in her spare time and didn't even care when the boys teased her for reading them. Plus, one of them was missing from her pile on Matt's porch table, and she was pretty sure it was either Jason or Easton who had stolen it. Imagining one of those burly bear shifters off in the woods, secretly reading a hot, erotic western romance made her laugh.

Something big moved across the river, and she jumped, startled. It was a massive grizzly, but she'd seen this one before. Matt had explained that the river served as a natural border between Gray Back territory and Boarlander territory.

"Hi, Harrison," she called to the Boarlander alpha.

The dark bruin gave her one last look, then ambled off into the brush.

"Geez, I'm never going to get used to that," she murmured as her heart rate settled. Or maybe she would if Matt would ever show her his bear. So far, he'd refused. In fact, she hadn't seen any of the Gray Backs' bears. Creed said it was a safety precaution around her, but Harrison never even bothered her when she was near the river. He just checked his territory line and moved on.

An hour passed like no time at all as she was lost in the imaginary world of Isla Homes, Bernard Duncan, and their romantic adventures through time.

"Do you regret not going to the beach now?" Matt asked.

With a grin and a bone-deep hum of relief,

Willa twisted in her chair. Matt was leaning against a tree, arms crossed over his broad chest, white T-shirt streaked with dirt, and speckles of mud all over his arms. At least today he wasn't bleeding, and after a week of him and Easton fighting, it felt like a victory.

"How long have you been here?" she asked.

"Not long."

"Hmm. No regrets. This week has been the best of my life. Besides, the beach has sharks, and I'm afraid of sharks, remember?"

"And deep water. And jellyfish, giant squids, hermit crabs, sea cucumbers—"

"Yeah, yeah, we've established I'm afraid of everything."

His bright blue eyes crinkled at the corners with his smile. "Everything except for bears."

She sighed happily and pushed off her chair. When she was snuggled in his strong arms, she admitted, "I missed you."

He rested his chin on top of her head. "I don't want you to go." It was the first time Matt had mentioned the looming end of her trip. He'd avoided it like the plague, probably because admitting she had to leave soon would make it real.

Willa squeezed him around the waist, then eased away and pulled his hand. "Come on."

Matt pulled his shirt off slowly, a troubled look in his eyes as she sank down in the water and waited. He was acting strange and distant, and she hated it.

"Do you have regrets?" she asked softly. The answer mattered more than anything.

He gave her the ghost of a sad smile and shook his head. "No." His abs flexed as he peeled off his jeans and kicked out of them. He was beautiful. A perfect Adonis. Perhaps other women wouldn't think so because of his striped skin, but Willa barely noticed that anymore. His scars and flaws were just a part of him.

"I wish my mom could've met you." Sadness washed through her at what couldn't ever be. "She would've liked you."

Matt dragged his legs through the waves until he reached her, then sank down until the water lapped at his chin. "You haven't talked about her before. What happened to your mom?"

"She died three years ago, just a few weeks after my Grandma."

"Jesus," Matt murmured sympathetically. He encircled her waist and pulled her deeper into the water. "Is your dad still around?"

"Yeah, he still lives in Minden." She scrunched up her face and swallowed the emotion that was clogging her throat. "If you can call it living. He's filled his house with pictures of him and my mom together when they were younger, and sometimes he talks like she's still around."

"It must be hard on you to see him like that."

"Yeah. She was sick for a long time, so I thought we were prepared, but when she went so close to Grandma passing, Dad just kind of shut down."

"Who did you lean on then?"

She shrugged her shoulders up to her ears. "No one."

The water babbled around them as Matt pulled her in closer and rested his chin on her shoulder. "I don't remember my parents."

This was it. Matt had kept his past carefully guarded since she'd met him, and this was the first time he'd even hinted at why he'd had to raise all those kids in the woods.

"I have this image in my head of them, but I think I've made it up. I imagine my mom as this tall, striking woman who talked in this powerful tone, and my dad as a quiet, silver-haired man with a straight back and strong shoulders, like mine. I really don't know what they looked like, though."

"Why not?"

"I was taken." He said it like a question, and his voice broke on the last word.

"Taken, like kidnapped?"

"The International Exchange of Shifter Affairs had this place they called the Menagerie. They picked up kids and...well, that's where I got my scars."

Willa's heart broke with his words, and she pulled him close so he wouldn't see the tears building in her eyes. "They did experiments?"

Matt swallowed audibly and nodded his head, spinning them in a slow circle in the water. "It wasn't so bad for me—"

"Matt," she warned. "I've seen your scars, remember?"

"It really wasn't, Willa. I'd been in there as long as I could remember, and at some point, I got used to the pain. It was just a part of my life, and I didn't know any better. But when I had to watch the other kids go in for tissue samples, it broke something in me. I was the oldest one there, and those kids felt like mine. Like my brothers and sisters to protect, and I couldn't do a damned thing. I was the only grizzly shifter, but they gave us medicine to stop our Changes. In the Menagerie, we only Changed when they let us off the meds, and in a controlled setting."

"A controlled setting?"

"Chained."

Fuck. Warmth streamed down her cheeks as she closed her eyes against the stabbing pain in her heart. "How long were you in there?"

"You're crying. I should stop."

"How long, Matt?"

Matt eased back. His eyes had gone dead, his face passive and emotionless. "Ages four to sixteen. Twelve years. I was Reynolds's first specimen."

"Reynolds was who you mentioned after you had that nightmare."

"He was the head of the Menagerie. He died a few years ago. I got to see it. He'd caught up to a couple of bears in the Ashe Crew, and the Gray Backs and Boarlanders came to help. Brighton and Denison Beck took him into the woods and put an ax to his neck. They took a kill I'd dreamed about my whole life. I was mad and relieved all at once. It dredged up a lot of memories, but it was finally over."

"Is this why your bear fights?" she asked, cupping his cheeks.

Another nod.

"Is this why you were searching for a mate?"

Matt wiped a damp strand of hair from her cheek. "Yeah. I thought it would fix me. Or at least make me feel more even—more normal. My sister found that with her mate, Haydan. I want that, too."

"Matt? Am I who your bear has chosen?"

Matt's face contorted, his eyes looking tortured as he leaned in to kiss her. Resting his forehead against hers, he nodded. "Yeah. You're my mate."

"Oh, Matt," she whispered, hugging him tight. How had everything got so screwed up? She'd known this—known there was something big happening between them. With every night they spent together, she felt the tether that bound their hearts thickening until it was unbreakable.

But this was supposed to be temporary. She was supposed to go back to her life in Minden, and if she was lucky, maintain a long distance relationship with Matt where she would visit as often as her new job allowed.

But this? Being his mate felt too big for long distance.

What was she supposed to do? She'd only met him a week ago, but this vacation felt more permanent now. More like home. But what could she do here? There were no job opportunities two hours outside of town, and she couldn't be one of those women who depended solely on a man to support her. She was too self-reliant for that, and someday, she'd grow to resent life here if it stole her independence. But now she couldn't even imagine saying goodbye to Matt for any amount of time. Not after he'd finally opened up to her and shared his painful past.

She had one day left with him before she had to make the decision to leave or stay. "I don't know what to do."

Pain pooled in Matt's sky blue eyes, and he kissed her again, harder this time. "I know," he rasped out before he ground his hips against hers.

Desperate to think of anything else, Willa nipped his bottom lip and kissed down his neck until that sexy growl she'd fallen in love with rattled deep in his chest. He pressed his long erection against her and grabbed her ass hard. Spinning her in the water, he pulled her back against him and slid his hand around her front into her bikini bottom. When he slid his finger inside of her, she groaned and arched back against him.

"You know how fucking hard it was for me not to bite you when you begged for it the other day," he growled against her neck. His teeth grazed her skin as he plunged his finger into her again.

Her breath came out in needy pants as she fumbled with the ties at her hips. The bikini slipped from her, and she threw it up onto the bank.

"I wanted to sink my teeth into your neck and force you to stay here with me. I wanted to give you a bear and tether you to the Gray Backs forever." He sank lower in the water, pulled his finger from her, angled her hips back, then slid his hard shaft into her from behind until she gasped.

Reaching back, she gripped the back of his head as he trailed kisses up her neck. "Please," she begged as he thrust into her again.

"Please what?" Matt cupped her sex with his palm and slammed into her from behind again.

Aw, hell, she didn't know. Couldn't think straight right now. Not when he was touching her like this. Worshipping her body, giving her what she craved. If he bit her, it would take away the uncertainty. She'd have to stay here with him. But if he bit her, she wouldn't be in control of her life anymore.

When she didn't answer, he stroked into her at a punishing pace, palm on her clit, shooting waves of pleasure through her nerve endings. She crashed back against him, blow for blow, gripping his neck as he clamped down on her neck with his teeth. Not deep enough to draw blood. Not deep enough to Turn her, but erotic enough to make her scream his name. Pressure built, and her insides tingled. Every thrust brought her closer to release, and Matt's hips were jerking fast now, as if he'd lost control. Usually he was gentle, but not today.

He shoved her forward through the waves until her knees hit the bank and her hands fell onto the sandy bottom. Waves lapped at her wrists and knees.

"Fuck," he gritted out as he bent over her, slamming into her from behind. He stretched her, filled her, brought her pleasure with a hint of pain. So big. Faster and harder until she exploded around him.

Squeezing her eyes tightly closed, she let

off a helpless yell. Matt slid into her one last time and froze, gripping her hips. Inside of her, he swelled and shot warmth into her in a pulsing rhythm, over and over until his cum trickled down her thighs and into the waves that rolled against her knees. Holy hell he was hot. Matt the gentle love-maker had been sensual and seductive. But Matt the man afraid of losing his mate, the man who'd just faced down his past to share it with her, the man who'd fucked her like an animal to let her body heal him, was sexy as hell.

She was boneless as he lifted her and dragged her back into the waves. He was quiet as he stroked her sex, washing her gently in the current.

I don't want you to go, he'd said.

After what he'd shared with her, and after finally exposing his primal side, she couldn't imagine leaving him.

She'd have to find a job in Saratoga, find an apartment, and get used to a long commute to see Matt and the Gray Backs. It would all be worth it, though, if she could keep this sense of belonging with the man she loved.

With a small kiss on the smooth skin of his neck, she whispered, "I'll stay."

TWELVE

Pain, pain, pain.

So scared.

Cold.

Skin tingling. Millions of needles. Can't breathe.

Sun hurts. Too bright.

Legs won't run!

Something big and terrifying growling. So close. Breathe!

Gasping, choking, vision blurs.

Woods, trees, sun too bright. Saturating everything. Turning it gold.

Hurts so bad.

Dying.

Roaring.

Roaring.

Screaming.

With a terrified gasp, Willa sat straight up in bed. Chest heaving and a whimper in her throat, she looked around. It wasn't dark anymore. It had to be midday. Head pounding, she felt her scalp to see if she'd split it, but there was no blood. Not even a knot.

So if she hadn't hit her head, why was she hallucinating that she was out in the woods?

Wake up, Willa. Wake up now.

She was completely naked, and her body was covered in cuts. She stared down at a long gash across her thigh that was shrinking by the second. "What the fuck?"

She was panting, breathing so fast she'd pass out if she didn't relax.

Birds called and cicadas sang in waves. Louder, softer, louder, softer. Branches creaked in the wind.

Wake up.

She stood and looked down at the bloody mattress in horror. Stained red, it was ripped up, exposing springs from the long, jagged gashes of something big. Why was her body covered in blood?

Matt's dream. He'd dreamed this, and now it was happening in her dreams.

A long snarl bellowed from her throat, and she sobbed in terror and searched the woods for the thing that was hunting her.

She felt sick. Her stomach was filled with something awful that didn't belong.

Stepping away from the bloody mattress, she stumbled on a tree root and fell hard on her backside. Air whooshed out of her lungs, and she couldn't suck it back in. She rolled from side to side, gasping. She wasn't supposed to feel pain in a dream, but her entire body ached. Cuts, scrapes, bumps. Her insides were burning.

The cicadas were growing louder until nature's song was deafening. The birds were bursting her eardrums. "Shut up!" she screamed, holding her hands over her ears.

Matt did this to you.

Willa froze and drew her first deep breath. No. He wouldn't have. He'd told her before they went to sleep last night that he'd never claim her like that. He liked her human, and that's exactly what she was. A human.

You can feel her in you—your bear.

No, no, no.

She stumbled upward and patted her face. Her glasses were gone but she could see every leaf, every pine needle, every bird in the trees, every color variation in the bark.

He wouldn't have. Matt cared about her.

He wouldn't do this.

But his bear was broken. He had told her it had been hard not to Turn her. Maybe he'd given into the temptation while she slept. She hadn't felt good last night and had gone to bed with him right after dinner with the Gray Backs. She'd felt woozy and sick.

Crying, she ran her hand over the blood that coated her shoulder. Her palm came back crimson.

This wasn't a dream.

"Matt?" she called to the unfamiliar woods. Another sob clogged her throat before she called his name louder. "Matt!" Her strangled voice dipped to nothing as she looked around. "Help me."

With one more glance at the ruined mattress, she sniffed the air. The intense smell of pine burned her nose and overpowered everything. Where was she?

There was no sound of running water, so she couldn't be near the river, and when she looked through the canopy above her, the mountains surrounding her didn't look familiar. The sun was directly above, and no help on direction. She needed to find a road or running water...something.

What if she was in Boarlander territory?

Fear froze her in place, and she began panting again. Harrison or any of his bears would kill her for trespassing.

Why had Matt done this? Why had he Turned her and left her to die alone in the woods?

Forcing her muscles to move, she stumbled off into the brush.

It didn't make any sense. Matt had made love to her last night. Been tender to make up for taking her hard at Bear Trap Falls. He'd been on the cusp of telling her he loved her. She'd felt it. And now this?

Creed had been right. The Gray Backs were broken and couldn't handle anyone outside of their crew. She'd just been too blinded by her affection for Matt to realize it.

Another snarl left her lips as the gravity of her mate's betrayal slipped over her shoulders.

Consequences be damned, she was going to kill him for what he'd done to her.

THIRTEEN

Matt hooked his hands on his hips and frowned at Willa's Tacoma, still parked by his truck beside his trailer. Where the fuck was she?

The hairs rose on the back of his neck, and when he turned, Easton was leaned against his truck, arms crossed, staring at him. Weird. Usually Easton spent his days off in his shack in the woods.

"Where's trouble?" Jason asked.

Willa had become a part of this place over the last week. It was really strange coming home to an empty house, and apparently he wasn't the only one who thought so. "I don't know. Maybe she went to the falls?"

"Why didn't she take her truck?" Jason asked.

Matt wondered that himself. Willa was too

smart to go wondering off in the woods alone, and the bombshells had left mid-week, so there was no way she hitched a ride with them.

The snap of a branch sounded from the woods, followed by a soft sob.

"Willa?" Matt called, instincts kicking up.

"Why's she crying?" Jason asked, trotting behind him.

"I don't know. Creed!" Matt called to his alpha over his shoulder.

Willa stumbled out from behind a tight grove of trees, and Matt skidded to a stop in horror.

She was naked and covered in caked, dried blood. Her dark hair was snarled, and she looked like she was having trouble walking, but that wasn't what had stopped him in his tracks.

Her eyes were churning an inhuman green color.

"No." His voice cracked on the word. "No!"

"Why?" she cried, stumbling toward him. "Why did you do this to me?" She was crying now, wailing as her shoulders shook with emotion.

"I didn't. I wouldn't." What the fuck had happened? Boarlanders? Ashe Crew? He was going to kill the mother fucker who'd Turned her. "Where were you?"

"In the woods." Her eyes narrowed to lethal slits. "In the woods where you dropped me on a mattress to bleed and shred it, just like your dream. You left me to wander these woods, lost and afraid for six fucking hours."

"I wouldn't. Willa, I swear I didn't do this."

"Liar!" she roared, the word tapering into a snarl.

"Whoa," Creed said, stepping beside Matt. His hands were out in a soothing gesture meant to calm wary horses. It seemed to be pissing Willa off more, though. "You feel that?" he murmured.

"Yeah, she's a fucking dominant," Jason said.

"She can't Change right now though, right?" Clinton asked from farther behind them where he'd stopped. He smelled like fear. "She's already Changed. She won't be able to do it again for weeks. Right?"

"No, she won't Change now," Creed said, stepping slowly closer to her. "Willa, we'll get everything figured out, but it wasn't Matt who Turned you. He was up on the landing with me all day."

A jolt of realization made Matt turn toward

Easton. "But you weren't. You were here all day with Willa."

"Wrong," Easton said, angling his head. "Willa was in the woods. I was in the trailer park, waiting for Willa to return."

"What the fuck are you talking about?" Matt gritted out.

"Willa was going to leave, but she can't leave. She's one of us now."

"What did you do?" Creed snarled.

"I did what Matt wouldn't. I made her one of us!" Easton's green eyes lightened to the same eerie color Willa's were now.

"You claimed my mate?" Matt yelled as fury blasted through him.

"I don't want your mate, Barns. I want her to stay here, with us, where she belongs. Now she will. She has no choice."

"You crazy sonofabitch!" Creed yelled, his voice cracking with power. "This right here is why I didn't want women up here. You can't fucking handle one. You don't even think you did anything wrong, do you? Look at her, Easton. Look at her face. Look at the blood on her. You did that. You *hurt* her."

Easton looked at each of his crew, then finally at Willa. His eyes darkened with uncertainty. "But now she won't hurt anymore. She'll heal fast. I took care of her. She's ours."

"You took my choice away from me," Willa whispered shakily.

The smell of rage was pungent against Matt's nose, and he dragged his gaze back to his mate. He'd never met a female bear who could wield as much dominance as was coming off Willa's skin.

"I had already agreed to stay. I didn't want to be a bear, but you put one inside me without my consent. Did you drug me last night?"

"What?" Matt asked, shocked by her question.

"I want to know if Easton drugged me," Willa roared. "I was sick last night. Did you put me to sleep so I wouldn't feel you drag me into the woods this morning? So I wouldn't feel you bite me?" A long, low growl rattled her throat as she glared down Easton, who could no longer hold her gaze. "Answer me!"

"Yes," Easton said, voice hitching. "I put sleeping pills in the drink I brought you at dinner."

"Willa, we'll figure this out," Creed said softly.

Oh, Matt knew exactly what his alpha was

feeling. The hairs on the back of Matt's neck were electrified, too. Beaston had created a beast in Willa, the stupid fuck.

"I'm going to kill you," she said in a growling, inhuman voice. She took a step toward Easton as he took a step back. "I'm going to bleed you like you bled me." Her eyes went vacant. "I'm going to dance to the song of your breaking bones, and if you're really, *really* lucky, I won't eat you until after you're dead."

"Willa, you aren't going to Change," Creed said in a careful tone. "It's too soon. You can't."

A long snarl rattled her throat, and she arched her gaze toward the alpha. With a slow blink, she allowed a dead smile to transform her face into something fearsome. "Wrong." An enormous brown grizzly exploded from Willa's skin. She landed on all fours, hard enough to shake the earth under Matt's feet. Eyes on Easton, she roared her death warning loud enough to rattle the trees and shake the birds from their branches.

"Run," Creed whispered. He dragged his wide, dark eyes to Easton. "Run now if you want to live."

****

Everything was bathed in shades of red.

Easton turned and ran for the trailer park, but he wouldn't make it far. Willa had longer strides and powerful new muscles that pushed her forward. Her claws dug into the dirt with each step.

"Willa, stop! You'll regret hurting him!" Matt yelled from behind her.

She'd regret nothing. Easton deserved to die. He'd forced her to Turn. Drugged her. Abandoned her in the woods, afraid and alone.

He'd made her into this...this...monster.

How could Matt love her now? He'd looked at her with horror in his eyes. A deep ache drummed through her as she pushed her legs harder. She was gaining on Easton now.

With a yell, Easton transformed into a silver grizzly. A true gray back. He spun right as she lunged for him, taking her full force in the chest. She ripped and bit and snarled and slapped. She raked her claws down his belly, slicing through skin and muscle until the air smelled like iron. He roared in pain and fought back in the jerky desperate moves of one who wanted to live. Stupid fucker shouldn't have killed her human then.

Something hit her side, bowling her against Creed's trailer. The wall splintered inward, and she brought her seething gaze to a brown bear that smelled like Jason. She charged, but he got out of her way. Easton was on the run, but he was no match for her. Not injured as he was.

Red, red, everything's red. Dead, dead, Easton's dead.

Another bear pummeled her in the side like a cannon ball. Legs splayed, she skidded across the ground, scrabbling across the chalky gravel for traction. Four bears against her, but Easton was on the ground now, and she was so close. Pain slashed across her side, down her ribs, and across her arms as the other bears fought and bit. She fought like a demon, clawing and hurting. She latched onto one of their necks and punctured him. Just a warning, she missed the artery on purpose. Next time she'd be more lethal. *Leave me the fuck alone.*

She reached Easton, but one of the bears knocked her legs out from under her. No matter, she could do damage from here. She latched onto Easton's kicking hind leg and bit down with all of her strength. The clean *snap* of his bone rattled her jaw.

Easton bellowed in pain.

A pitch black bear hovered over Easton, teeth bared. Smelled like Creed. He roared a warning and a wave of power brushed her skin. Made her bear focus. He was trying to tell her something. Something important. *He* was important. Boss. Alpha.

She shook her head, uncertain.

Easton was bad. He was a bad bear. Bad.

But...he'd been nice to her before. Back when she was human. Gifted her a knife. Smiled at her after he came home from work with the others. Got mad at Jason for teasing her too much. He'd defended her. He'd made an effort to spend more time with the crew because she'd asked.

Not a bad bear.

A broken bear.

Like her.

Closing her eyes, Willa tucked her bear back into her skin. It hurt. Her bones ached too much to hold her weight, so she sagged to her knees in the dirt with a sob. She looked down at her arms, covered in claw marks and puncture wounds. Everything hurt.

She looked up at Matt's bear, a scarred warrior, dark as a redwood and pacing tightly in front of her, between her and the other bears. Protecting her.

He'd told her once that no one else bled like Gray Backs.

She looked down at her crimson arms and lost a vital part of herself. The part she'd been clinging to that this was all just some nightmare, like the one Matt had endured. She lost hope that this could be fixed. That *she* could be fixed.

No one bled as much as a Gray Back.

And now she was a Gray Back bad bear.

Standing on shaky legs, she looked down at Easton, who screamed as he Changed back. He was shredded, clawed up, and gritting his teeth in pain.

"Dude," Jason said, looking beat up and bloody. "I can see your intestines."

Creed shrank back into his human skin. His neck had a claw mark down it, and she felt like grit.

"That's what he fuckin' gets," Creed muttered.

"Set my bone," Easton pleaded. "His leg had been snapped in half, and a jagged, white shard stuck out of his knee.

Clinton moved toward him, but Creed halted him. "I should kill you, Easton. It's against shifter law to Turn people without consent. You claimed your Gray Back brother's mate. You are no longer in contention for second or even third. You were just bested by a brand new sow. Willa is second in the crew now, if she chooses to stay with us. Her true mate, Matt, is third. That's not your real punishment, though." Creed angled his head as his eyes narrowed to dangerous slits. "Your punishment is resetting your own bones."

"I can't," Easton panted. "I can't do this one. It's too bad."

"Then you shouldn't have fucking Turned her!" Creed roared. The alpha jammed a finger at Clinton. "I forbid you to set his bones." He turned to Jason. "I forbid you to set his bones." He gave the same order to Matt, who was still a red, scarred-up bear. And at last, he turned to Willa. His voice went hoarse. "This is the way our world works, Willa. I can tell from your face you want to help him, but grizzly shifter law is in place for a reason. He was wrong. He shouldn't have hurt you. Easton's punishment is a permanent limp to remind him of what he's done to you. I forbid you to set his bones."

Easton let off pained noises with every breath now.

Willa couldn't look at him. "I'm sorry," she whispered to him, tears streaming down her face.

Unable to bear the sound of his agony

anymore, she ran for the woods, for the falls. For the first place she'd been when she visited these mountains. She was dirty on the outside and in. The only thing that could wash her clean was Bear Trap Falls.

The ground was uneven and stung the bottoms of her feet with cuts, but she didn't care about that now. She'd heal in no time. All she cared about was getting as far away from Easton as she could.

He'd hurt her, Turned her, but she'd hurt him back. The sound of his snapping bone echoed through her mind, over and over. Tears blurred her vision as she stumbled through the woods toward the distant sound of running water.

Faster and faster she ran until the forest morphed into a smear of brown and green. She could run forever now and not get tired. Her bear pulsed inside of her, relieved to be away from the others and in the woods. The woods felt like home. *These* woods felt like home.

A sob tore out of her as she skidded to a stop on the bank of the river. "I'm a monster."

"No, you're not," Matt said from behind her.

Oh, she'd known he was following. She'd

sensed him and heard him. He hadn't tried to follow quietly.

She turned, and he caught her, clutched her hard to his bare chest.

"You're not a monster." His voice sounded raspy, as if he were forcing the words through his tightening vocal cords. "You're so fucking beautiful. Your bear is perfect. Strong and fierce, just like you, Willa." He picked her up and carried her into the water, then washed the blood from her arms. From her face and neck as she cried silent tears.

"How will I tell my Dad?"

"I'll help."

"How will I tell my friends?"

"The bombshells? They'll be insanely jealous. And if they don't like it, you can eat them."

The first hint of a smile curved his lips.

With a sigh, she traced the long, open gash across his shoulder. "I hurt you."

Matt snorted. "I've had worse. You were terrifying and lethal. Powerful. Do you know how rare you are?"

She frowned and hugged his neck as he walked along the sandy bottom toward the falls. "What do you mean?"

"Did you not hear Creed declare you

second in the crew?"

"I don't know what that means."

"It means you are second only to the alpha. Easton and I have been battling for that rank for two years. It's why I always come home bloody."

"Oh no, I took your spot? I'm sorry." Shit, she couldn't do anything right.

"Nerd, I'm glad you took it. I don't care about rank. It's a dominance thing with our bears, and your bear is a beast."

Chills rippled up her arms. "You say that like it's a good thing."

"I just watched my mate whoop Easton's ass. That was fucking awesome. I wanted to kill him." Matt gritted his teeth so hard a muscle in his jaw twitched. "I wanted to rip him apart limb from limb for what he did to you, but I didn't have to. You can defend yourself just fine."

"You don't think the boys are going to be mad at me for...you know..."

"Taking every one of us on? No, not mad. Shocked, but not mad. You just dumped our little crew on its ass, Willamena Madden. And you came damn close to taking this crew out from under Creed."

"I wanted you to do it," she rushed out.

"Do what?" he asked, touching her cheek just under her eye.

"I thought about this, Turning. I imagined what it would be like years from now if we decided to do it. I know you didn't want to Turn me, but I thought if I was ever like you, it would be because you chose me."

"Oooh, Willa," he whispered, stroking a damp tress of her hair from her face. "I already chose you. I just didn't want you to have to register to the public. I didn't want you to ever go through what I did with IESA. I wanted to protect you."

"So you regret that I'm like this?"

He shook his head, his blue eyes so sad. "No. If anything, I love you more."

She smiled through her tears. "You love me?"

"I do, and I can't stand that Easton was the one who claimed you."

"Will you fix it?"

Matt nodded uncertainly. "It'll hurt." He brushed his fingers over the uneven skin of the scar Easton had bitten into her shoulder.

"Do it quick. I don't want to be Easton's."

Matt's throat moved as he swallowed hard, and he turned her gently in the water. She exhaled a shaky breath as he laid a kiss over her claiming mark. This would seal their linked fates. His bite would tether their lives together for always, and a trill of excitement blew through her as he kissed her scar again, grazing his teeth against her this time.

"You ready?" he asked in a gravelly, sexy voice.

The cicadas died down as if they anticipated the life-altering moment. The frogs and birds didn't sound as deafening as she prepared to receive the mark that would change the course of her future. Toes on the sandy river bottom, water lapping at her breasts, gooseflesh on every inch of her body, she nodded. "I'm ready."

Matt's teeth sank into her shoulder. Burning, blinding pain consumed her for a moment as he clamped down and cut into muscle, and then he released her, and the ache lessened. Cleaning her gently with river water, he told her, "You're mine now, Willa, and I'm yours. I'll protect you from now until the end of my life. I don't have much, but you can have all of it. All of me."

She relaxed back against him as happiness flooded her veins. *I don't have much.* He had more than enough for her.

Matt kissed her earlobe and opened his

mouth to say something more, but someone whooped and splashed into the water right beside them.

Jason popped up near Willa and grinned. "Hey Gray Back Badass."

She washed the tears from her cheeks. "More like Gray Back Bad Bear."

"Please," he muttered, kicking away with a splash. "All Gray Backs are bad bears. Wear that title with pride."

Matt laughed from behind her and splashed Jason. Clinton swung from the rope swing and tucked his body into a ball. His canon ball wave dumped over them. When he came up for air, he said, "Hey, remember that time this girl no bigger than a kid turned into a monster bear and kicked all of our asses?"

"I told you," Creed said from where he was sitting on the beach. "C team."

"Not C team anymore," Clinton argued. "Everyone will be jealous. If Willa is part of our crew, we have a dominant badass chick to add to our already substantial awesomeness."

"Who can cook gumbo," Jason added with a teasing smile.

The boys seemed happy, excited even, but she'd only been a bear for half a day and had just tried to kill and eat one of their own, like a psychopath. Sarcastically, Willa muttered, "You're all so lucky."

"We are," Easton said from the trees. He was leaning heavily on a towering spruce, his eyes averted.

If she didn't have her new bear hearing, she would've missed his soft admission.

"Better get a towel on if you don't want everyone to see you naked," Creed called from the shore where he held up what looked like a cartoon turtle beach towel.

"Hate to break it to you, but everyone has already seen me naked. No use in hiding my teeny ta-tas now."

"Yes, our crew has, but unless you want the other crews to see you, I'd suggest you hurry scurry. I've called our friends and they live close."

Matt grinned and kissed her, then swam her to the bank and carried her out of the water.

"What friends?" Willa asked.

"You'll see," Matt whispered against her ear.

Creed settled the towel around her shoulders and sighed. He gripped her shoulders and slowly pressed his forehead against hers. "Welcome to my crew."

Clinton, dripping wet with a grin on his face, did the same and pressed his forehead to hers. "Welcome to the Gray Backs."

Jason followed. "Welcome to the new A team, Gray Back Badass."

Matt kissed her forehead for a long time. "Welcome home…" His smile lifted his lips, then faded. "Mate."

She gripped his wrists and squeezed her eyes tightly closed, absorbing the hope she'd thought she'd lost. Maybe she wasn't broken after all. Maybe she could be a better version of herself here, if she worked hard enough.

She turned to Easton, who hadn't moved from his place by the trees. From the way he was hunched over in pain, he likely couldn't move well. Approaching slowly, she hoped he didn't hate her.

"You said you were sorry for hurting me," he murmured as she squared up in front of him.

"I am."

He looked up at her, green eyes full of remorse and sadness. "It's I who am sorry, Willa. I didn't realize it was wrong. I liked that you were nice to me, and I didn't want you to go away. My selfishness hurt you. I'm sorrier than you'll ever know."

Willa tried to smile, but she was too emotional. "Welcome me home then, and I'll think about forgiving you someday."

Tenderly, Easton, her maker, stood straight and cupped her face. Leaning his forehead against hers, he whispered, "I welcome you home, Second." He eased back and angled his head at a crowd of people traveling up the bank of the river. "Now go on. You have more people to meet."

Baffled at the large number of people gathering by Matt, she padded toward them. A blond-haired woman stood at the front, tears rimming her eyes. "Is it true?" she asked Matt thickly. "Have you found her?"

Matt nodded and pulled Willa against his side. "Cassie, this is my mate, Willa. Willa, this is my sister, Cassie."

The woman pulled them both in close. She was crying, shoulders shaking with quiet sobs. "I always hoped he'd find you."

Willa sniffled and hugged Cassie and Matt tighter.

Cassie eased back and wiped her damp cheeks with the back of her hand, then gestured toward the crowd behind her. A pair of women were sniffling and smiling kindly, and a tall man with striking blue eyes shook

Creed's hand, while a little bear cub and a little girl chased each other through the crowd. Another man was holding a box of red wine. Each one of them looked different, but they all wore similar, welcoming smiles on their faces.

Matt clapped the back of a dark-headed man with tattoos up his neck, then turned to her. "Willa, newest member of the Gray Back Crew, meet our allies, the Ashe Crew."

As Matt led her to each of the Ashe Crew to introduce them, and then through the Boarlanders and the Lowlanders, Willa was awed at what she'd stumbled onto here.

These people, these crews, were like families, and she'd chosen hers in the Gray Backs the day she'd fallen for Matt. And even though she was scared and had a lot to learn about her bear and this new world she'd fallen into, she was proud to be here. To be a part of a crew. To be second to Creed, and Matt's chosen mate.

The claiming mark on her neck tingled as Matt gripped her shoulder and hugged her close.

She was safe and alive and wanted.

But more than all of that, she belonged.

As long as she lived, she'd have a crew at her back. People to protect and care for.

People who would protect and care for her.

The bombshells' purpose suddenly became so painfully obvious. She'd had to endure unhealthy friendships to appreciate what she had here.

"Are you okay?" Matt asked, looking down at her with worry in his eyes.

"Better than okay." Pushing thoughts of painful past friendships away, she smiled up at him, her loyal, adoring, scarred and imperfect, but always patient mate. "I think I'm going to like being a Gray Back."

Want More of the Gray Backs?

The Complete Series is Available Now

Up Next

Gray Back Alpha Bear
(Gray Back Bears, Book 2)

About the Author

T.S. Joyce is devoted to bringing hot shifter romances to readers. Hungry alpha males are her calling card, and the wilder the men, the more she'll make them pour their hearts out. She werebear swears there'll be no swooning heroines in her books. It takes tough-as-nails women to handle her shifters.

Experienced at handling an alpha male of her own, she lives in a tiny town, outside of a tiny city, and devotes her life to writing big stories. Foodie, wolf whisperer, ninja, thief of tiny bottles of awesome smelling hotel shampoo, nap connoisseur, movie fanatic, and zombie slayer, and most of this bio is true.

Bear Shifters? Check
Smoldering Alpha Hotness? Double Check
Sexy Scenes? Fasten up your girdles, ladies and gents, it's gonna to be a wild ride.

For more information on T. S. Joyce's work,
visit her website at
www.tsjoycewrites.wordpress.com

Made in the USA
Middletown, DE
13 March 2017